WHERE
the RIVER
TAKES US

Books by Lesley Parr

The Valley of Lost Secrets
When the War Came Home
Where the River Takes Us

WHERE the RIVER TAKES US

LESLEY PARR

BLOOMSBURY
CHILDREN'S BOOKS
LONDON OXFORD NEW YORK NEW DELHI SYDNEY

BLOOMSBURY CHILDREN'S BOOKS
Bloomsbury Publishing Plc
50 Bedford Square, London WC1B 3DP, UK
29 Earlsfort Terrace, Dublin 2, Ireland

BLOOMSBURY, BLOOMSBURY CHILDREN'S BOOKS and the Diana logo
are trademarks of Bloomsbury Publishing Plc

First published in Great Britain in 2023 by Bloomsbury Publishing Plc

A catalogue record for this book is available from the British Library

ISBN: PB: 978-1-5266-4777-1; Waterstones: 978-1-5266-6530-0;
eBook: 978-1-5266-4778-8; ePDF: 978-1-5266-4776-4

2 4 6 8 10 9 7 5 3 1

Typeset by RefineCatch Limited, Bungay, Suffolk

Printed and bound in Great Britain by CPI Group (UK) Ltd, Croydon CR0 4YY

To find out more about our authors and books visit www.bloomsbury.com
and sign up for our newsletters

For Angharad

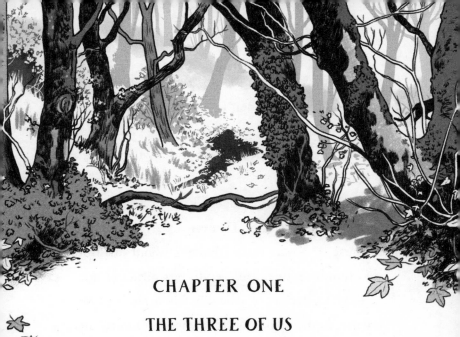

CHAPTER ONE

THE THREE OF US

It's surprising how many people in a small town will believe there's a wild cat on the loose. Up the valley, in Blaengarw, loads have seen it, but no one has real proof.

Funny that.

Jinx thinks it's true – but then, he would. He's over by the old brick shed on the other side of the waste ground with Tam, collecting stuff to build a bike ramp. But I'd rather bomb around, spraying little stones into the air when I spin into skids.

This place, this scruffy, gravelly patch of land covered in rubble and pallets and anything else that can be dragged here, is where most of us Ponty kids hang around after school. I know everyone and everyone knows me. I never used to mind that, because I never really thought about it. But it's different now. Because everything's different now.

I try to perfect a wheelie, hit a stone, lose my balance and land on my side, wheels spinning. Just as Catrin comes over the top of the hill, hood up against the wind.

She runs over. 'Jason! You okay?'

'Yeah,' I say, rubbing my arm. Good job my parka's nice and thick.

'If you want to ride on one wheel, why don't you get a unicycle?' she asks, holding out a hand, but I get up without taking it.

'Choppers are cooler.' I grin, checking my bike for scratches.

All around us, kids shout and play. Some younger ones run past with their coats buttoned at the top like capes, yelling the *Batman* theme tune; on a tower of old car tyres, a girl's pretending to be a teacher, bossing her friends around; most of us older ones are on bikes. It's better than the park; that's got flower beds and benches and grown-ups.

This is just for us. This is ours.

'Why are you so late anyway?' I ask Catrin.

'Flipping bus broke down,' she says. 'Again. Wish I could walk to school like you.'

I look down the road, behind her. 'Where's Rhodri?'

'Left him outside Harwell's, drooling over the Airfix kits. Mam's going to tell me off, but I've got tons of homework.' She lifts her satchel, like she's trying to prove there are loads of books inside. 'Little brothers are a pain.'

'I bet that's what Richie says about me.'

'He's doing his best, you know.'

I shrug. 'Suppose.'

Catrin shuts up. That's the great thing about her.

She knows not to give me the look, the *I'm sorry your mam and dad died and your brother has to look after you* look. I get it from everyone else; teachers, Aunty Pearl, even Jinx and Tam sometimes. That's me; Jason North, the Ponty Orphan.

I hate it.

Jinx rides over and Catrin goes kind of stiff. They've never got on. Jinx has this thing about me, him and Tam being 'the three of us', so he doesn't give her a chance. And Tam's Tam – all for a quiet life – he never chooses sides. But Catrin's been my best friend since her family moved in next door when we were tiny. Everyone knows it.

'You're bleeding.' Jinx looks down at my knee. 'Give me a look.'

'No, you weirdo!'

'Hey, guess what?' He points to some kids chalking hopscotch on the pavement. 'We were just talking to them, and there's been another sighting of that wild cat. A man from Craigwern got a photo of its tail.'

I raise my eyebrows. 'Its tail?'

He waves Tam over. 'It's true, isn't it, about the cat in Blaengarw?'

Tam pulls up next to us, blocking out the low winter sun – he's massive, Tam is, gets it from his rugby coach dad. 'Yeah,' he says. 'People reckon it's too big to be a pet.'

'They all say that though.' I turn to Catrin. 'You agree with me, don't you?'

She screws up her face. 'To be honest, Jason, I'm not sure. I mean, why would all those people lie?'

Jinx claps his hands together, then holds them out in a *See what I mean?* sort of way. 'Exactly!'

Hang on … Did he just agree with Catrin?

He looks into the distance, eyeing the mountains above the houses. 'Imagine if it was here instead of Blaengarw. We'd find it. Easy.'

Catrin scuffs her shoe on the ground and smirks. Jinx's too busy scanning the fields to notice. 'It's a puma or a jaguar, I bet you.'

'I know what type of cat it is.' They look at me like

they're surprised. I lean forward, my eyes going from side to side like I'm watching for spies. 'Imaginary.'

Catrin laughs and walks off. 'See you after, Jason.'

Jinx watches her go. 'Why does she have to come here anyway? Everyone knows the waste ground is for Ponty kids.'

I shove him.

He glares at me. 'Leave off, Jase, mun!'

'She *is* a Ponty kid though,' Tam says. 'She just goes to the Welsh school, that's all.'

'Yeah,' I say. 'And you don't own the waste ground. If you did I'm pretty sure you'd ban those two.'

Another bike flies past us, the rider and person on the back screeching and shouting like maniacs – Gary Hall and Dean Bolan. They bomb out on to the road, not even stopping to check for traffic.

Tam turns his bike. 'Last one to the ramp has to marry Mrs Fletcher!'

I jump on my Chopper, no way I'm getting there behind Jinx.

They've built a really good ramp out of an old door

and some bricks. Tam has the idea of laying corrug-
ated iron in front of it so when we ride over the top it
just about shakes our brains out.

'We could come back tomorrow and make it a full
assault course,' he says. 'I reckon my father will let us
have some old training equipment we can make into
jumps.'

'Brilliant!' Jinx checks his watch. 'Let's get it higher
now, before it's too dark. I'll fetch more bricks.'

'Can't,' I say, turning my handlebars. 'Got to get
home.'

'All right.'

They never argue any more, never try to persuade
me to stay out longer. Because they know I have to
make tea.

Standing on the pedals, working them hard, I ride
up the hill to my house.

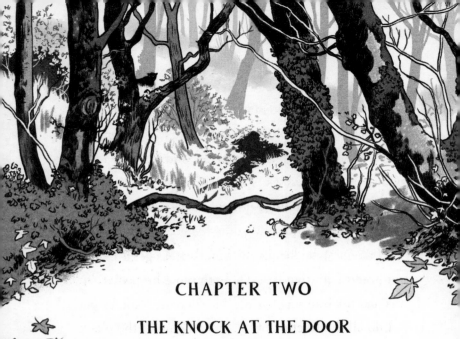

CHAPTER TWO

THE KNOCK AT THE DOOR

It's not easy to chop a potato by candlelight. I've cut my finger twice. Finding a plaster in the messy drawer isn't easy either, but I've washed the blood off the chips. Richie won't know. I'm trying to make this candle last, like he said I had to, but how he expects me to do that, I don't know. Not without sitting in the dark.

On my own.

Waiting for him to get in from work.

I thought the blackouts would at least mean no homework. No such luck, and the way Richie goes on about wanting me to have better choices than he has, he'd probably set me some himself anyway.

He's stricter about it than Mam and Dad ever were. He used to do my sums for me then. And he was fun. Now he keeps on about being my *guardian*, so I have to do what he says. I preferred him when he was just my brother.

I do all the fractions first, glancing up at the clock every now and again. He's late. It's nearly six. Where is he? We have to cook tea at six on the dot, because that's when the power comes back on. I sneak the last Bourbon out of the biscuit barrel to keep me going, then turn over the page, dreading the decimals I know will be there.

The key rattles in the lock, the front door opens and closes, dragging over the loose bit of carpet we never find time to fix. Richie appears in the kitchen doorway, arms wrapped around himself, foot jiggling up and down like he's twitchy about something. I suppose it's work again.

'All right?' He squints through the gloom. 'Done the chips, have you? Good boy. Won't be long now and we can get the pan on. Sorry I'm late.'

'Where've you been?'

He washes his hands in the sink; in the dark window, his reflection frowns. 'Talking to Dai Dep. Work stuff. Nothing for you to worry about.'

I was right then. I still worry though. Less work means less wages, and we were only just making the mortgage payments, even before the three-day week. It's all because there are miners' strikes, and something going on in the Middle East which I don't really understand, but it means the government can't get enough coal and oil to run things so they're cutting the power and making some people work less days.

He reaches into the bowl, pulls a slice of raw potato from the water and takes a bite.

'Aww, Jase, mun, you haven't got all the skin off! Again.'

10

'You try peeling spuds in the dark,' I say. 'Anyway, it won't matter once they're fried – more goodness in the skin, isn't it?'

'Whatever you say.' He reaches into the fridge for a pack of sausages. There's a buzzing and a flicker and the kitchen light comes on. Soon, we're tucking into bangers, chips and marrowfats.

'How was school?' he asks, taking another slice of bread from the tower between us. We always have lots of white sliced; it's cheap and fills you up.

'All right. Same as usual. Boring. Oh, but!' I bite my chip butty. 'Jinx said—'

'Don't talk with your mouth full.'

I chew fast and swallow. 'You sound like …' But I can't finish the sentence. The word gets stuck.

'I sound like her, don't I?' He speaks quietly, as if the words will break if he says them too loud. He reaches inside his jumper. He does it all the time, without thinking, and rubs his thumb over the St Christopher pendant Mam and Dad got him for his eighteenth birthday.

I nod.

He smiles. It's not real. He takes a big breath, leans back in his chair. 'So, come on then, what's Jenkins said now?'

He always calls him Jenkins, not Jinx. Probably because Dad did.

'You know that big cat people say is up Blaengarw?'

Someone bangs on the front door so loud we jump.

He pushes his chair back. 'I'll get it.'

I pack more chips into my fat butty and take another bite. Lovely.

Richie's speaking low and fast. 'I told you not to come here.'

I get up to see who's there. It's Snook Hall – what the hell's he doing here? Richie steps on to the pavement and closes the door behind him.

This can't be good.

I rush down the passage and press my face to the wood, trying to listen. I can't catch much, but I do hear 'tonight', 'not a request' and 'money'.

What the hell is going on?

The door clicks open, just a bit, and I leg it back down the passage and into my chair. When Richie comes back in, he's got his coat on. He leans over the table piling chips, peas and a sausage on to a slice of bread, then puts another one on top.

'Got to nip out. Won't be long.' He ruffles my hair like I'm five. 'You'll be all right for a bit, won't you?'

I stare at him.

'That was Snook Hall!'

'Leave it, Jase.'

'*Snook Hall*, older brother of Gary, Jinx's mortal enemy.'

'Don't be so dramatic, mun.'

'What did he want?'

'Nothing for you to worry about. Got to go. You can tell me about that big cat when I get back, yeah? We'll wash up together – all tidy for when you-know-who comes tomorrow.'

Aunty Pearl, as if I could forget. But I'm not letting him change the subject.

'Snook mentioned money – you don't owe him, do you?'

'It's nothing like that.'

I stand too. *'Tell me.'*

Richie reaches across and puts his hand on my shoulder. 'Forget it, eh?' His voice is softer now. 'Your big brother's got everything under control.'

Then he's gone, leaving me here with a sick feeling.

I can't stand this. I need to know what's going on. I slam my knife and fork down and run out of the house. I catch him before he reaches the corner of our street. He spins round when he hears my feet thudding on the pavement.

'Jason! What the … ?' His face changes – goes from surprised to worried. He looks like Dad. 'Where's your coat?'

'Where's my coat? Is that all you can say?'

'It's cold.'

I stare right at him. 'I might be thirteen but I'm not stupid. I've had to grow up fast, remember.'

Richie runs a hand through his hair. He looks down

at his feet, then up at me from under his eyebrows. He blows out a long breath.

I'm hopping on my toes now. 'I'll follow you. You can't stop me. I'll—'

'Jesus, Jase, okay!' he says, eyes darting everywhere. 'Not here though, eh?'

He takes his lumberjacket off and puts it on me. We walk through the streets, just sort of wandering. He eats his butty and I wait. Even though it kills me, I wait for him to speak because I can't push it. Not now.

'I made a bad choice,' Richie says, tapping his chest where the St Christopher is. 'A really bad choice, and now it's got worse.'

My mouth goes dry. 'What sort of choice?'

'I stole diesel from the depot.'

'You *what*?'

'To sell to Snook Hall.' Richie blinks and looks into the darkness towards the mountain. 'Not much but it was tidy money. He said it was a one-off and it paid for that last sack of coal we had. But then Snook

15

wanted more from me. See, his gang was looking for a welder. To help patch up all the cars and parts they've been stealing.'

My brother. A thief.

I swallow. 'And you said yes? Are we that poor now?'

'Honestly, Jase?'

'Honesty would be good, yeah.'

But he looks like a nervous little boy and suddenly I'm not so sure I want the truth.

Richie puffs out his cheeks. 'I don't think we can make the mortgage this month.'

He shoves his hands deep in his pockets, his shoulders all hunched like the weight of the world is on him, which I suppose it is, and my heart aches for him, and for me.

What a mess we're in.

'I was worried about my wages going down and got myself in a bit of a state. I wasn't thinking properly.' He holds his hands up. 'No excuse, I know! But Snook's crafty, they were never bothered about diesel, the plan all along was to hook me in. Have something to hold over me. So they started making threats—'

'Is that why he came round?'

Richie nods. 'And to get me to do extra tonight or they'd make sure everyone knew I stole the diesel. Then I'd have no wages at all.'

'How much do we need for the mortgage?'

'Each repayment is twenty pounds. I've got about half that.'

'And if we don't get it?'

'We'll have it. You've got to trust me, Jase.'

Only the tips of my fingers peek out from the sleeves of his jacket. I can't stop staring at them. 'But … if we don't, we can't stay together, can we? If we have no house. Social Services, they'd make me live with Aunty Pearl.'

'I reckon, yeah.'

'But …' The words stick in my throat, so I do a little cough. 'If you go to jail, we won't be together either.'

'I'm not going to jail.'

'How can you—'

'It's just till we get over this three-day-week nonsense. Get the mortgage paid on the first, and hopefully by next month things will be different.'

Does he really believe that?

'I know this sounds twisted, but I'm doing it for us.' He smiles, but it's sad. 'Now, give me my jacket back and clear off home, eh? I shouldn't have told you …'

'I didn't really give you a choice, did I?'

I put my arms around him and squeeze really tight. He squeezes back.

'It'll be all right,' I say. 'We're in this together now.'

He lets go and holds me at arm's length. 'No, Jason. We're not. Not this. This is my problem and you can't tell anyone else. Not Catrin, not the boys, no one.'

'Course I won't,' I say, already knowing it's a lie.

In bed, cwtched up under the blankets, I point my torch at *Look-in* magazine, but it's hard to flick through the pages with gloves on. Richie told me to use the Calor Gas heater and stay downstairs, but I'm not wasting fuel. With my bobble hat on as well, it's not too bad. I lean my head back on the pillow and stare at the ceiling. I didn't think things could get any worse after Mam and Dad died, but here I am on my own in the dark while my brother is out breaking the law to keep us together.

The 1st is next week. St David's Day – usually a good day. Except now it's mortgage day, a day to dread.

For someone who has to be the grown-up, Richie's doing a really bad job of it.

And I've never felt more like a useless kid.

CHAPTER THREE

THE BEAST OF BLAENGARW

'Jaaaaason! Jaaaaason! Jaaaaason!'

I leave my Sugar Puffs going soggy in the bowl and go out the back where Rhodri's waving something over the garden wall.

'It's a Tiger Moth!' He wobbles on the old milk crate he uses to see into our garden and makes the Airfix plane zoom around in the air. 'It was in the war.'

'It's great,' I say. 'Can I hold it?'

'Yep.' He hands it to me. 'See the two cockpits? The pilot goes in the *back one*!'

'Wow.' I hand it back. 'Where's your sister?'

'In the kitchen. Shall I fetch her?' I expect him to get down and go inside but instead he bellows another ear-splitting shout. 'Caaaaatrin!'

Nothing.

'Caaaaatrin!' The back door opens.

'God, all right! What is it now?' she asks, coming to the wall.

Rhodri grins. 'Your boyfriend wants you.' He jumps off the crate and runs up the garden, through the back gate on to the lane, making aeroplane noises all the way.

'Wally.' She pulls a face. 'Take no notice.'

'I'm not,' I say. 'His new plane's good.'

'I wouldn't know, he won't let anyone near his models, except you.'

'What you doing?'

'Colouring. I've got some new felt tips. You can use them if you don't press too hard.'

21

'Not now. Got to go food shopping, fancy coming?'

'Gwyn's or Co-op?' She pushes her hair behind her ears, showing the scar by her left eye.

I look away. 'Gwyn's.'

'I want to pick up my magazine, so yeah.'

We call Gwyn's the corner shop, but it's at the end of a terrace really. It's a funny shape, with the door right on the end so there's always a squeeze on the pavement. And it gets really busy on a Saturday morning; kids spending pocket money, old dears gossiping, men looking at papers, weighing up the betting odds. Next stop the bookie's, then the club to watch the races over a pint.

Dad never did that. He used to take me and Richie for walks up the mountain. *Let's get you out of your mother's way*, he'd say. *Give her a bit of time to herself.* Mam loved it because she had some peace and we loved it because we had Bloke Time. Even when I was tiny, we called it that. Me and Richie used to say we'd always have Bloke Time. Even when we were grown up and Dad was old, we'd push him around Ponty in a wheelchair.

But that'll never happen now.

Jinx and Tam are outside Gwyn's. Their heads down, reading *The Herald* – the local rag. What are they doing with that?

'Jason!' Jinx says, waving a page in front of my face. 'Look at this!'

I push it away. 'I can't look at anything if you shove it right at me. What's in there that's so interesting anyway?'

Tam grins down at me. 'Money.'

'What?'

'A reward,' Jinx says, his eyes all daft and goggling like a cartoon person. 'Look!'

I take the paper and they crowd round me. Catrin's immediately pushed out, so I elbow Jinx out of the way so she can see too.

BIG CAT SIGHTING REWARD
£100 for clear, exclusive photo
See bottom right for Terms and Conditions

'And?' I say. 'What's it got to do with us? The cat – if it exists – lives up Blaengarw. That's miles away.'

'Yeah, but we could go,' Jinx says. 'Between the three of us it's just under thirty-three pounds fifty each; I worked it out. Imagine what we could do with thirty-three pounds fifty, what would you buy? I'd get …'

I want to say about six weeks' mortgage, but I don't.

He keeps on, ignoring the fact we don't even have a camera, getting stupidly excited about trekking up the valley, finding a wild beast and being in the paper, but I've stopped listening. It's all right for him and Tam, their families have money – they're not rich – no one around here is rich – but they have enough so their kids can dream about spending prize money on treats. They don't have to think about food shopping and boring, boring bills.

And they don't have to worry about dodgy blokes like Snook Hall knocking the door.

'Oh, look out,' Tam mutters.

Gary Hall and Dean Bolan are crossing the road

towards us, doing that stupid, swaggery walk they think makes them look tough.

'Oi, Jinxy-boy! Lend us three p,' Gary says. 'I need matches.'

Jinx stares at the paper as if he hasn't heard. He's always nervous around them, which I get, because they pick on him the most, but he's safe with Tam here. Which is weird, as Tam's never had a fight in his life – just the size of him is enough for Gary and Dean to not push things too far.

'Gone deaf or what?' Dean pokes him in the back.

'I haven't got any money left,' Jinx mumbles.

'Leave him alone,' I say.

Catrin's eyes flick from me to Dean. Tam, as usual, just folds his arms and says nothing.

'What's this then?' Dean leans over my shoulder. 'Oh, the Beast ... my uncle saw it last week.'

'Yeah, right,' I say.

'You calling him a liar?'

I shrug. 'Well, if he can prove it, he gets one hundred quid. There's a reward in here.'

'*What?*' Gary whips the paper out of my hands and reads the page. 'We'll have this, thank you very much.' He folds *The Herald*, puts it under his arm and they go off down the road.

Jinx glares at me. 'Why'd you have to go and tell *them*?'

'What difference does it make, Jinx?' I say. 'There *is* no flaming cat.'

Catrin follows me into Gwyn's and pretends not to notice when I stock up on the reduced, dented cans.

It's not far, but the bags are heavy so we have to keep stopping. At the end of our road, a woman's coming towards us, trundling her tartan shopping trolley.

'Fletcher alert!' Catrin whispers. 'Pretend we're deep in conversation, she might not try to talk to us then.'

Fat chance of Ponty's biggest stirrer doing that, but I say, 'Okay.'

Which, of course, means that now we can't think of a single thing to say before Mrs Fletcher reaches us.

'Been shopping, have you?' she asks. 'That's what I'm doing now. Getting the bus into town. Better shops in town, see.' She stretches her neck to look in my bags. 'Those spaghetti hoops – half-p cheaper in Tesco, they are.'

My fingers close around the handles of the bag, blocking her view. 'Only cheaper if you've got a bus pass, isn't it? Otherwise the fare cancels it out.'

Mrs Fletcher's lips go tight. 'Well, I'm just trying to help.'

'Anyway.' Catrin pulls herself up very straight. 'We like shopping at Gwyn's.'

'I'm only saying. Must be hard for Jason and Richie being on their own.'

Catrin pulls on my sleeve and we try to get past, but Mrs Fletcher hasn't finished. She puts on a simpering look, leaning down, talking in that fake-gentle voice people like her always use to show the world they care. 'How are you, boy? Is it getting any easier? How long's it been now? Eight … ten months?'

My stomach twists into a messy knot, my throat

feels tight. I need to get away.

'We're going now,' Catrin says, her voice strong and hard, like steel.

Mrs Fletcher doesn't even look at her. She leans closer, her voice soft but her eyes hungry, like she hopes I'll break, start crying in the street, so she can go and tell all her friends down the bingo about the poor, sad boys whose parents died in that car crash on Emmerson Road and how she's such a good neighbour, looking out for us. 'Dreadful business, both of them going like that. You must miss them something awful. I remember when our Billy got knocked down ...'

Catrin gasps.

Billy? Billy was her *dog*!

Hot and cold waves ripple all over me. If I stay here I'll explode. I drop the bags, push past the stupid woman and run, fast, up our street, past our front door. I keep going, across the next road. Brian Carter's workshop is dead in front of me, the metal shutters down. I don't slow, let myself slam into them, shoulder first, and crumple to the ground. Breathing hard. Seething hard. Hating Mrs Fletcher with all my might.

I wrap my arms around my legs and press my head into my knees, hot tears soaking through my jeans. I don't know how long it is until I hear footsteps. Someone stops in front of me. I open my eyes, move my head slightly and see blue-and-white trainers. Catrin doesn't say a word, just sits down next to me. For one weird second, I think she's going to put her arm around my shoulders but all she does is sit right up close. And I let her.

After about ten minutes she says, 'You don't usually let Mrs Fletcher get to you.'

I finally look at her, turning my head to the side and wiping my cheeks. 'Billy, mind!'

'I know,' she whispers.

But Catrin's right. As usual. It's more than that. It's the horrible feeling I've had in my chest ever since Snook knocked our door. So I tell her about Richie and Snook's gang and she listens. Then we don't say anything for a while, and it feels okay to have said it all. Good, even. Because, with Catrin, I can admit I'm scared witless.

She plays with her shoelaces, pressing the little plastic ends into her palms, making marks. 'My mam's going to kill me.'

'Why?'

Her face scrunches up. 'Because of what I said to Mrs Fletcher.'

CHAPTER FOUR

AUNTY PEARL

Richie's trying not to laugh, I can tell. 'She called Mrs Fletcher a *what*?'

'You heard,' I say, passing him a clean, wet plate. 'And the old bag went straight next door and I don't think Catrin's going to be allowed out again till she's thirty! Anyway, shut up, mun, Aunty Pearl will hear you.'

We look at the ceiling, knowing she's upstairs, scrubbing the bath like a mad woman. She's not our real aunty, she's Mam's godmother. Catrin's aunties are young and trendy, and she loves them babysitting her and Rhodri. Aunty Pearl is more like a grim old nana.

But Richie's still grinning. 'I didn't think little Catrin Rees knew words like that.'

'It's not funny,' I say. 'She won't even be able to speak to me over the wall. Remember when we were six and we took those flowers off that grave? It'll be like that.'

'*Took?*'

'Okay, we robbed them – but only to give to Catrin's gran!'

He finishes drying the plate and puts it in the cupboard, sniggering to himself.

'Stop laughing!' I snatch the tea towel and flick him with it. 'We *meant well* –' flick – 'and Catrin's gran was landed! –' flick. We play fight, until he surrenders. And it feels great, like things used to be.

But the feeling goes away fast when Aunty Pearl appears in the kitchen doorway, face like thunder; big and terrible in the brown checked overalls she wears *to keep her clothes nice.*

'We're only messing about,' I say quickly.

'So I see.' She folds her arms. 'Aren't you a bit old for that, Richard?'

He looks at the floor and tries to hide his words in a cough so only I can hear. 'Apparently not.'

'Don't, Rich,' I mutter.

Sometimes it's best to keep quiet and let her get on with it, but he can't seem to do that.

'I've tidied your bedroom, Jason,' she says.'Got rid of those old magazines in the box next to your bed.'

'*What?*' I sound a bit shrieky. 'I was reading them!'

'Oh, don't be silly, they're out-of-date. The ones at the bottom had 1971 written on them!'

'That's because I *collect* them!'

'We've asked you not to go in our bedrooms, Aunty Pearl,' Richie says, his voice whispery, like he's trying to keep his temper. 'Where are they now, his magazines?'

'In the outside bin. But I really can't see what the

fuss is about.' She starts emptying the washing machine, not looking at him.

'No,' Richie mutters. 'You really can't, can you? Don't worry, Jase, *I'll* get your magazines.'

Aunty Pearl gasps. 'Out of the bin?'

'Yes, because that's where you put them. Without asking.' He stops on the back doorstep. 'Then I'm going to watch *World of Sport*.'

She turns to me. 'I hope you never speak to your elders like that.'

'Richie's all right,' I say.

She raises her eyebrows and makes her lips really small as if I'm simple and she's the wise woman of the flaming valleys.

'It's time he grew up and started shouldering his responsibilities.'

How much more grown up does she want him to be? Mostly it feels like a thousand years since Richie North could be anywhere near irresponsible, the cool kid everyone wanted to be mates with. But he's doing his best – we both are. If she stopped judging and picking and sniping for five minutes, she'd see that.

'We look after each other,' I mumble.

'That's just it though, Jason. A thirteen-year-old boy shouldn't be looking after his nineteen-year-old brother. He's the man of the house now.' She closes the washing-machine door. 'And if the state of the bathroom was anything to go by, I don't think he's doing a very good job.'

The bathroom? She really doesn't get it.

'We look after each other,' I repeat, firmer this time.

Aunty Pearl huffs, grabs the wash basket and goes out to the line.

But I know what she's getting at. She *wants* him to mess up. She's been circling like an old buzzard for months, saying I'd be better off with her. Making out like he's completely rubbish at being my guardian. And she treats me like a little kid. Always fussing over me, blaming Richie for things, even when it's my fault. Like the time I got a really low mark in my spelling test; she said Richie could have helped me learn my words. And when Jinx accidentally split my head open with a skimming stone and I had three stitches; she reckoned Richie should *keep an eye on the company I keep*.

God, imagine if she knew the company *he's* keeping! She'd never understand that he's doing it for us. If he went to jail, it'd suit her just fine. Then she could be right.

I kneel on my bedroom floor, putting the magazines back in the right order. Why does she have to mess everything up? Stupid, interfering old bat. The muffled voices downstairs get louder, only the odd word drifting up to me until …

'The boy has holes in his clothes!'

Aunty Pearl's off again.

'He fell off his bike yesterday.' Richie fumes. 'Kids do! We've got a patch for it. You make it sound like he's walking around in rags!'

I go and twty down at the top of the stairs, holding on to the banister like prison bars.

'Don't say *kid*, Richard. He's a boy, not a baby goat.'

'*Oh my God!*'

'All I'm saying is …' Her voice stays calm. 'You need to think about the future – for both of you.'

'*I. Am.*' Richie's nearly shouting now. 'It's all I flaming well think about! The future! And bills! And making sure Jason's okay! And – oh forget it. Why am I even trying to make you see? What's the damn point?'

Oh no, that's a Class A swear word to Aunty Pearl, that is. She's chapel.

'Well, Richard, you need to think a bit harder, good boy. Don't – don't you dare walk away when I'm speaking to you.'

The back door slams. I rush to my bedroom and go straight to the window to see Richie pacing the garden, clenching and unclenching his fists. She won't follow him out there. The last thing Aunty Pearl would do is row where the neighbours could hear. She says it's common.

I slump on to the floor. Flipping Aunty Pearl.

Always thinking we need her help. Well, me and Richie are fine without her.

Except ... we're not fine. Not really. And we can't fix it on our own.

I look up – at the mountains all around our valley and the road which leads to Blaengarw.

Maybe we don't have to fix it on our own.

I've got mates. Good ones. Mates with a wild idea and just the right mix of stupidity and determination to pull it off.

CHAPTER FIVE

NOT CHARITY CASES

'I'm in!' I yell, speeding across the waste ground and pulling my brakes so hard I nearly go over the handlebars.

Jinx swerves away from the ramp and rides over. 'In what?'

'Looking for the big cat. I want to do it.'

Tam joins us.

'You'll come on the quest?' Jinx grins. 'Brilliant!'

'The *what?*' me and Tam say at exactly the same time.

'The quest. For the Beast of Blaengarw.'

We burst out laughing.

'What?' Jinx asks, holding up his hands and laughing too. 'A quest is when you search for something, seek it out. Looking for the cat is a quest.'

'If you say so,' Tam says. 'But I'm more interested in why Jason's changed his mind.'

I glance around. Too many kids – including Gary and Dean, who have already started to demolish our ramp, but that doesn't matter now. 'Not here,' I say. 'Blue Bridge.'

We ride through the streets to the river. The Blue Bridge is our place, where we dangle our legs and skim stones and make fires to bake spuds. We leave our bikes on the bank and go on to the smooth pebbles that make a kind of beach.

'Richie's in trouble,' I say.

'What kind of trouble?' Tam asks.

I screw my face up because my mouth doesn't

want to let the words out.

'What kind of trouble, Jase?' He sounds really worried now.

We sit in a little huddle. 'Snook Hall's got this thing going on with stolen cars and …' I lower my voice, even though there's no one else here. 'They needed a welder. Richie's doing it.'

'No way.' Tam folds his arms. 'No way your brother would be involved with that scumbag.'

'Yeah,' Jinx says. 'Who told you that?'

'Richie.'

They stare at me like a pair of thickos. Then Tam blows out a long breath.

Jinx shakes his head. 'Oh, man.'

I tell them about the wages cut and the mortgage and Aunty Pearl. I tell them how Richie's leaving me on my own to work for Snook. But I only tell them the facts, not the feelings. The facts are enough for these two.

Jinx stares into the distance; he does this when he's thinking hard. 'I know!'

'Know what?' Tam asks, frowning.

'Richie's doing this for the money, yeah?'

I nod, feeling awful, like I'm a traitor to my brother or something. But I'm desperate.

'Well ...' Jinx leans in closer. 'If it's all about the money, then you'll need more than thirty-three and a half quid. Sooo ...' He stares at Tam and raises his eyebrows. 'What do you reckon, butt?'

Tam looks at him with a well-used *What are you on about now?* expression. After a few seconds, he sits back and nods slowly. 'Oh, I get it. We don't share the hundred quid between us.'

And I get it too.

I want to say no way. That me and Richie are not charity cases. But I think of the alternatives – him in jail, me moving away to live with Aunty Pearl, losing my friends and my brother as well as my mam and dad – and I nod.

My voice comes out all scratchy. 'I'll pay you back.'

'No need,' Jinx and Tam say together.

I look hard into their faces. *'I'll pay you back.'*

They glance at each other, then nod.

I do a little cough to make my voice smoother. 'A hundred quid would buy us time. It's five months' mortgage and the three-day week might be over by then.'

'It will,' Tam says. 'It can't go on forever. But our biggest problem is still the camera. Or *lack of* camera.'

'Karen's got one,' Jinx says. 'An Instamatic, had it for Christmas.'

'Your sister will never lend us her brand-new camera to take up Blaengarw on some mad expedition,' I say.

'It'd be no use anyway,' Tam says. 'We need a big, posh one with a telephoto lens – you know, one that zooms in and out.'

'Sounds pricey,' I say.

'Put it this way, if we had money for all that gear, we wouldn't need to look for a giant wild cat.'

We sit quiet for a minute. All racking our brains.

Jinx says our comp has some fancy cameras, but they don't let pupils take them off school grounds unless it's a proper trip, and its half term anyway, so we're scuppered before we even start.

Me and Tam take the mick out of him for using the word 'scuppered', but, whatever we call it, we're still no closer to solving our problem. We decide to go to Jinx's to put our heads together. His house has the best biscuits.

CHAPTER SIX

THE MAP

Jinx pours us a glass of squash each. 'Have a look at that,' he says, over his shoulder.

On the kitchen table, next to a pile of library books, is a map. I unfold it and lay it out flat.

'Is this our valley?' Tam asks as we sit.

'Yeah.'

'Why do we need a map?' I ask. 'We know how to get to Blaengarw, just follow Top Road.'

45

'It's not as simple as that,' Jinx says, digging around in the biscuit barrel. 'We need to use the river path.'

'Why? Top Road's faster.'

'Yeah but we need to keep out of sight as much as we can. We're not going to tell the *truth* about where we're going, are we? Our parents would never let us go all the way to Blaengarw to look for a wild animal.' He stops, turns to face me. 'Sorry, Jase. I didn't think, I'd never …'

'It's okay,' I mutter, fighting with the empty feeling creeping over me.

'It's not though.' Jinx looks like he just stepped on a puppy. 'I didn't think. I—'

Tam cuts in. 'Show us this map then.'

He won't look at me. He never looks at me when this comes up. Jinx might say the wrong thing sometimes, but at least he *says* things. Tam acts like my mam and dad never existed.

Jinx takes a big breath. 'Right.' He smooths the map with his hand. 'The good thing is it's the holidays, so we have more time. As long as we get to here –' he runs a

finger along a thick, red line on the paper – 'and here …
by sunset each day – that's five o'clock – it'll all be okay.
We don't want to be travelling in the dark, especially
with the blackouts. And I've picked out sheltered places
to sleep so we don't even need to carry a tent. Look.'

I look closer; the red line is in felt pen. Jinx has
planned our route in detail.

'It's almost all path,' he goes on. 'But there are some
parts where it stops because the mountain's so close.
Then we have to cross at certain places – mostly
bridges – but also some stepping stones just past the
Nant Copperworks.'

He fetches our squash and Penguins. 'But we need
to get our backsides up there ASAP – there'll be
others wanting to get a photo.'

Tam swigs his squash and then splutters. 'What
the heck is this?'

Jinx shrugs. 'Pineapple. I know, I know – my
mother's going all exotic. But it's either that or water.'

Tam pulls a face. 'I'll drink it.'

I have to admit, even though we usually take the

mick out of him for being so organised, Jinx's way is the best way to do things. By the time his mother kicks us off the table to make tea, we've learned quite a lot:

About why a map is divided into squares – me and Tam never have paid attention in Geography;

that Blaengarw is eleven miles away, but the twisting river path makes it sixteen;

that the average thirteen-year-old should cover three miles per hour;

and that pineapple squash is a crime against taste buds.

Jinx's mother makes hot dogs and lets us eat them in the living room. They're brilliant, like the ones from the fair – with fried onions and lots of red sauce and mustard. Tam thinks he's in heaven; at his house he always has to sit at the table, even for snacks.

'About the camera,' Jinx says. 'We'll take my rubbish old pocket one and hope we can get close enough for a good shot.'

Me and Tam have to agree. Got no other choice. Although I don't fancy getting *too* close to a wild beast.

'Do you think we'll be allowed to go?' I ask. Jinx and Tam look at me like they don't get what I mean. 'It *is* February.'

'It's *unseasonably mild* though,' Jinx says. 'What? Don't laugh. It's what the weatherman said!'

'God, you're a wally.' Tam shoves the end of a hot dog into his mouth.

Jinx ignores him. 'Tam's dad already reckons winter camping builds character, and you know my mam and dad let me do whatever I want.' He wiggles his little finger. 'Got them wrapped round this, haven't I?'

'Yeah and we're not telling them we're going all the way to Blaengarw, are we?' Tam says. 'Just to our usual spot.'

I pull a long bit of onion from my roll. It's like a delicious, crispy worm. 'I reckon Richie will go for that.'

Catrin's dad's coming down Cae Terrace as I walk up. 'All right, boy?'

I nod.

'I'm glad I caught you,' he says. 'Look, I hope you don't think I'm sticking my nose in but, well, me and Bethan, we care what happens to you and Richie ...'

I scuff the ground with my shoe. Here we go – more people trying to look after us.

Nigel carries on. 'Richie's not hanging around with Snook Hall, is he?'

'Why would he be doing that?'

'I don't know. You tell me. Dai Dep thought he saw them in Snook's car, up on Esgyn Road.'

'Thought he saw?'

He blows out a long breath. 'Yeah. Yeah, you're right. Dai just probably needs his eyes checking or something.'

I fake a smile. 'Yeah.'

'That's what I told Bethan, but she asked me to check, so ...' He wrinkles his nose, looking just like Catrin. 'It's only because—'

'Yeah, I know.'

You care. Everyone flipping cares. That's what happens when you don't have parents any more. Sometimes I

think it must have been easier in Victorian times, you just got shoved in an orphanage and forgotten about.

Richie's upstairs when I get in. He pops his head over the top of the banister. 'Nice tea at Jinx's?'

'Lush. Hot dogs.'

'With onions again?'

'Yeah.' I take off my parka.

'Lovely, mun.'

'Can I go camping this week? With Tam and Jinx.'

It's like he's not really listening. 'Er, yeah, if you want.' He comes down the stairs. 'Bit cold though, isn't it?'

'We'll wrap up.'

'All right then.' He takes his coat off the stand. 'I'm glad I've seen you now, saves me leaving you a note.'

I don't even bother asking where he's going, because it won't stop him. But soon – because me, Jinx and Tam have our plan – things will be different.

He gives me a quick cwtch. 'Love you, see you later.'

'Love you,' I whisper back as the front door shuts with a click. 'You stupid idiot.'

CHAPTER SEVEN

TITCHY LITTLE PEBBLES

I can't sleep. I'm lying here, in the dark. Holding my breath every time I think I hear the door. It's almost eleven and Richie's still not home.

Drrr!

A shower of hard things hits my bedroom window. I sit up.

Drrr!

What the hell? Sounds like hailstones, big ones. I

get out of bed and open the curtains. The moon and stars are bright in the sky. No clouds at all. So what's …

Something hits the window again and I jump. Now, looking into next-door's garden, I see a spooky face lit from underneath by a tiny torch.

Catrin.

She waves her arms to show she wants me to come down. I pull on my dressing gown and slippers and rush through the house and out the back. Her torch is off now, but the clear night means I can see her well enough.

'What are you doing?' I whisper.

'Checking you're all right,' she says, pulling the collar of her dressing gown up.

'Erm, I was till someone started chucking rocks at my window.'

'Don't be so twp,' she says. 'They were titchy little pebbles.'

'What's up?'

She leans on the top of the wall, resting her chin on her arms. 'I already said – checking you're all right.'

She's always like this. Fussing about me. The weird thing is, when it's Catrin, I don't even mind.

'You mean Richie?'

'It'll be okay,' she says. 'He's not daft.'

I look up at the dark shapes of the mountains looming over the terraced rooftops and almost laugh. 'Then he's doing a very good impression of a daft person.' I sigh. 'It's not all bad though. Jinx thinks if we can get a photo of the big cat – even if it's only with an ordinary camera – we can get the reward.' I wait for her to say it's a crazy idea, that Jinx is an idiot, but she just frowns and nods for me to go on.

'Him and Tam say ...' I fiddle with the belt on my dressing gown. 'They say me and Richie can have it all so he can walk away from Snook's gang.'

'That's kind,' she says quietly.

'He's not as bad as you think he is, you know. Jinx.'

'So you keep saying.'

'Not sure how much of a chance we have without a posh camera, but ...'

Catrin chews on the inside of her cheek for a second. 'I might—'

There's a distant noise like the jangling of keys.

'Oh heck,' I say. 'Is that Richie?'

She stares at our house.

Sounds come from inside and I see the glow from the gas lamp. Me and Catrin duck down fast. *Oh God, did I shut the back door?* Yes, I must have, to keep the cold out. I think …

The tap turns on and off with a clang. Richie must be having a drink of water.

Please go up without checking the back door. Please go up without checking the back door. It might not be the coldest February we've ever had, but I don't fancy sleeping in the coal bunker.

The lamplight moves away. My heart thuds like crazy.

'I have to post some letters for Mam in the morning,' Catrin whispers. 'Meet me outside the post office at half eleven.'

She flicks her torch back on and rushes inside.

CHAPTER EIGHT

PENTAX SPOTMATIC SP500

Catrin's already by the postbox. She grabs my arm and pulls me along the road. 'Come on. I haven't got long.'

'Where are we going?'

'Are Tam and Jinx down by the Blue Bridge?'

'Suppose so.'

'Then that's where we're going.'

When we get there, they're skimming stones. Me

and Catrin race across the bridge, making it judder and clang. On the other side, we run down the bank and come to a stop on the pebbles.

'All right?' Tam says. 'I got one to the other side in three skips.'

'I did a sevener once,' Catrin says. 'As far as that tree it went.' She points downstream.

Jinx folds his arms. 'Oh, *did* you?'

'Yeah,' I say. 'She did. I was with her.'

I wasn't, but I'm not having Jinx make out like Catrin's lying. She glances sideways at me and smiles.

'Well,' he says. 'I did a niner once, didn't I, Tam?'

'No idea,' Tam says, rummaging around for another flat stone.

'Well, I hope that made you feel very special,' Catrin says.

My laugh comes out like a snort.

'What's up? Tam asks, lining up his aim. 'You don't usually come down here, Catrin.'

'It's about the big cat,' she says, looking really excited. 'I've got a good camera, a *really* good camera.'

Jinx is horrified. 'You told her!'

I give him a *Shut it or else* look.

Tam frowns. 'What sort of camera?'

'It's a Pentax.' She glares at Jinx. 'A Spotmatic SP500, 50mm with a wide-angle lens. Think that'll do the job?'

'Where'd you get that from?' I say quickly, before Jinx can react to her sarcasm.

'My dad had it for his birthday,' she says. 'Remember, Jason? He made a big fuss about wanting a special present for his fortieth but I don't think he's even taken it out of the box.'

'And he'll lend it to us?' Tam asks.

'No, but he'll lend it to *me*.'

'But that means you'll have to … Hang on … no way!' Jinx yells. He looks from me to Tam, wide-eyed. 'No way is she coming on our quest!'

Catrin sighs. 'There won't be a quest if you don't have a decent camera.'

'We don't need your dad's stupid Pentax,' Jinx says.

'I think you do. Or you could take yours and hope

the Beast likes you enough to come nice and close. Or – I know! How about taking your crayons up and doing a nice drawing of it?'

Me and Tam laugh.

'This is for Jason and Richie,' Jinx says.

She puts her hands on her hips. 'I know. Which is why you need the best chance. My dad's camera gives us that.'

'How come you're even allowed? Whoever heard of a girl going on a boys' camping trip?'

'Not all of us have parents in the Dark Ages! I'm allowed because Jason will be there. And he's my—'

Tam chucks the stone down so hard it splinters, making us all jump.

'Catrin's coming,' he says. 'No decent camera, no decent chance.' We all stare at him. 'But you two better find a way to get on because if you think I'm putting up with this rubbish all the way to Blaengarw and back, you can think again.'

Jinx huffs loudly. 'All right, mun!'

Thank God for Tam. I didn't want to have to get in the middle of *that*. 'So, when do we go?' I ask.

'Tomorrow,' she says. 'First thing.'

'You're not in charge.' Jinx seethes.

I turn to him. 'When do *you* think we should go then?'

He pushes some stones around with his foot and mumbles. 'Tomorrow.' He looks up. 'But I was going to say it first! None of this is *her* idea, remember!'

Idiot.

I look around at them all and I feel excited for the first time in forever. Like I can do something to help Richie instead of just peeling spuds and buying dented tins of spaghetti hoops from Gwyn's.

We're really doing it.

We're going up the valley to find the Beast of Blaengarw.

CHAPTER NINE

SETTING OFF

Me and Catrin meet on the pavement outside our houses. She hoicks her rucksack on to her shoulders and grins. 'Ready to find a cat?'

'Ready.' I grin back.

We've just set off when her front door opens and Rhodri appears in his pyjamas and slippers. He's swinging two flat, round things by their straps. 'You forgot these!'

Canteens – like the ones soldiers have.

'I didn't know you had those,' I say.

Catrin takes them from her brother. 'They're from the Army and Navy Store. Dad got them for him and Rhodri.'

'Make sure Jason has that one,' Rhodri says, pointing to the one with an *R* embroidered on to the strap. He looks up at me. 'It's my one.'

I smile at him. 'Thanks.'

'Wish I could come with you.'

I shrug. 'Maybe you can do something nice with your friends.'

He does a big, over-the-top sigh. 'I suppose. Not camping though.'

'Look,' I say, putting a hand on his shoulder. 'When we're back, I'll take you swimming, just you and me. What d'you reckon?'

He nods, then gets a funny look on his face. 'Do you know what name Catrin called Mrs Fletcher? No one will tell me. Mam just said it was shaming.'

'Nice try,' I say. 'Now get inside before you freeze.'

'And back to bed!' Catrin says, already walking away. 'It's only half six.'

We lug our rucksacks down the hill. It's so quiet. All we can hear is the hum of the milk float as it turns on to Cae Terrace.

'Not right though, is it?' I say. 'That Mrs Fletcher can say what she likes because she's a grown-up, and we can't.'

'Oh, don't worry, Dad told her straight. Said she needs to start minding her own business. That I shouldn't have said what I said, but I was provoked.'

'Did he really?'

Catrin nods. 'I heard him tell Mam.'

'Your dad's brilliant.'

'He said he was trying to see it from our point of view. But Mam said that's bound to be easier for him as he's a big kid anyway.' She smiles. 'He *is* brilliant though; he sneaked me up a Caramac. I had to stay in my room, see.'

'No telly?'

'No telly,' she repeats. 'But the power went out

again anyway, didn't it?'

I pat the bobble on her hat. 'You're a top mate, you are.'

Gwyn's opens really early for the papers, so we stop to buy supplies. People who go on expeditions have something called Kendal Mint Cake; Nigel says Ernest Shackleton took it to the South Pole. But Gwyn doesn't sell that so we get a few packs of Polos and a quarter of midget gems.

Tam and Jinx are already at the Blue Bridge when we get there, the map held out in front of them.

'All right?' I call.

They look up and wave.

Jinx folds the map and looks at Catrin. 'Let's see this camera then.'

She takes a leather case out of her rucksack, undoes the clasp and pulls out the camera. I reach for it but she holds it close to her.

'Okay,' she says slowly. 'But put the strap around your neck first. And be careful, it's heavy.'

It is too. You can tell it cost a lot of money. 'What does this do?'

She takes the lens cap off; it hangs down on a little cord. Then she shows us what all the buttons are for before taking out another case and unzipping it. Out of that comes a lens which she screws on to the front of the camera. 'This is what will get us a good shot.'

When the camera whirrs and the lens comes out like a stubby telescope, me, Tam and Jinx go *Ooh*, as if we're at the fireworks.

Even Jinx is impressed. 'That's tidy, mind, fair play.'

Catrin smiles, but down at the camera, not at Jinx.

'I'm the only one who can use it though,' Catrin mutters. 'My dad said.'

'What?' Jinx whines like Rhodri. 'That's not fair!'

Tam tells him to shut it and we set off along the path we know so well. Heading for ones we don't. We've walked right up to Ystradmawr before now. One summer holiday, that was. But mostly we don't go further than a few miles.

'If one of us had a dog, then we'd be like the Famous Five,' Catrin says. 'Going off on an adventure.'

'Aren't two of them girls?' Jinx asks.

'Yeah,' Tam says. 'That'll be Catrin and Jason then.'

I hit him because that's what I'm supposed to do. But really, I don't see what's so bad about being a girl; Catrin seems to like it.

CHAPTER TEN

BREAD OF HEAVEN

We get to the place where we can see the rugby club across the river. I remember when Jinx's cousin had her eighteenth there. Me and Tam were allowed to go because his mam and dad thought it would keep him out of trouble. Only it didn't quite turn out like that, because we decided it would be funny to go around supping the dregs out of people's glasses when they weren't looking.

67

We were only nine. It was bad.

Tam fell asleep in the corner of the ladies' lounge under a pile of coats and no one could find him for ages. Jinx got on a table and sang 'Bread of Heaven', and I threw up over his gran.

Me and Tam catch each other's eye and start singing:

'*Bread of heaven, bread of heaven, Feed me till I want no more …*'

'Very amusing,' Jinx says, pulling a face. 'Remind me to laugh next time.'

'*Feeeeed me till I want no more.*'

Clapping comes from somewhere on Top Road. We look up, past the trees, to see Gary and Dean.

'Beautiful voices,' Gary says, clapping again. 'You should join the school choir.'

'Get stuffed!' I shout.

Dean clocks our gear. 'Going camping, are you?'

'None of your business.'

Catrin tilts her head and mutters, 'They've got rucksacks like us. You don't think they're looking for the Beast too, do you?'

'Surely not,' Tam says.

'What about you?' she shouts up the slope.

'Us?' Gary yells. 'Same as you by the look of it. Going to Blaengarw to get rich.'

Oh, man.

'We don't know what you're on about,' Jinx yells.

'Yeah you do,' Dean says. 'But you might as well go and camp in your back garden, Jinxy-boy, because *we're* getting there first and *we're* getting that photo. So long, suckers!'

They flick us the Vs and walk off, laughing.

Jinx groans. 'They'll get to Blaengarw first if they're on Top Road.'

'Then we'll just have to get a shift on,' I say, hoicking up my rucksack.

'Yeah,' Tam says. 'Use the opposition as motivation. That's what my dad always says.'

Catrin smiles. 'Your dad's right. Come on.'

We head for the viaduct, imagining what kind of cat it could be. Jinx still thinks it's a puma, but me and Catrin say panther. Tam reckons it's a lynx. Jinx, of course, now thinks he's an expert after reading those few library books.

It's mid-morning when we reach the viaduct, and the sun's warm enough for us to take off our bobble hats. I unzip my parka. We sit on our rolled-up sleeping bags under one of the huge, stone arches.

'Let's see what food we've got,' Tam says.

I turn to Catrin. 'He loves his grub. Once, at his house, we had bangers and mash and he ate six bangers. *Six*, mind.' I raise my eyebrows to emphasise what a big deal that is.

'Yep.' Tam grins. 'Only six … had to leave room for afters.'

Me and Catrin laugh but Jinx just frowns into his rucksack.

We lay it all out. Me and Catrin packed together and our things look like picnic food; sandwiches, crisps, sweets, and some pasties and sausage rolls that Bethan made. Tam's brought some bread rolls, baked beans, tinned hot dogs for us to have over the campfire tonight, bacon for the morning, and Cup-a-Soups and fruit. Much more like camping fodder than ours. But Jinx has pulled everything out of his rucksack and is rummaging in the bottom, a look of panic on his face.

'What's up?' I ask.

He says nothing, just keeps scrabbling about in his bag.

'Oh God, you haven't forgotten your food, have you?' Tam says with a groan.

Jinx turns to face us. 'I thought I'd put it in but I must not have. It's on the kitchen table. I can see it now.' He holds out a white box with a green cross on it. 'I remembered the first-aid kit though.'

'Oh, well done!' Tam says. 'Bandages on toast tonight then!'

'I thought you said he was really organised,' Catrin says to me.

'I am!' Jinx squeaks. 'I can't be expected to do everything, can I? I've researched the cat, planned the route, worked out all the timings, got the first-aid kit.'

'Yeah, you said,' I mutter. Typical Jinx. His grandfather's a doctor, so he thinks he knows about medical stuff. He's brainy, but he's not *that* brainy.

'Well, none of *you* thought to bring one!' Jinx's voice gets louder. 'And you'll be grateful I did if you have an accident and end up with your leg hanging off!'

'Yeah, because we can stick it back on with plasters.'

'All right, mun!' Tam says. 'We're hardly out of Ponty and you're arguing. Look, there's plenty of food, we'll just have to share more, that's all.'

'And have less,' I say.

'There's enough so shut up, Jase.'

I shut up.

Jinx pulls out a small pair of binoculars. 'And I brought these.' He glances at Catrin. 'They're not fancy or anything but they do work.'

Tam takes them off him. 'Are these toy ones?'

Jinx snatches them back. 'No. They're just small.'

I'm pretty sure they are toy ones, but no one else brought any and they'll be better than the naked eye, so fair enough.

Tam opens a big bottle of limeade and raises it in the air. 'Keep the village alive!' He takes a swig, then passes it to Jinx, who gives it a good wipe with the end of his sleeve before having some and saying the toast. Then I do the same.

Catrin says she'll drink her water.

'That canteen is cool,' Tam says. 'Very cool.'

She smiles and unscrews the cap. 'What's that about?' she asks. 'Keeping the village alive?'

'It's what the blokes down the pub say. It means to keep your spirits up.'

'Oh, okay.' She looks at her canteen for a second, and I wonder if she's thinking about saying it but she just drinks.

Jinx rummages in his bag again. 'I remembered this though!' He holds up a toilet roll. 'And if you want to take the mickey out of that, then you can use leaves and I hope they give you the world's itchiest rash.'

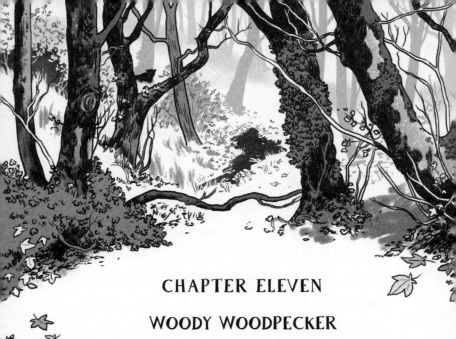

CHAPTER ELEVEN

WOODY WOODPECKER

Just past the viaduct, the path narrows so we have to go in single file. I walk at the back, thinking about why we're doing this. Richie wasn't an angel – that's part of what made him so cool – but he never would have bothered with Snook Hall when Mam and Dad were here; he hated that type of lad – rough and mean and sneaky. But they seem to be the only people he hangs round with these days. If his mates hadn't got fed up of him not being able to go down the pub, maybe they'd have stopped him. Suppose they weren't really good mates at all. Not like mine.

There they are, up ahead of me. Tam leading the way, Jinx whacking at anything he passes with the great big stick he found. And Catrin, in her padded anorak, turning every now and again to smile at me.

A tapping sound comes from the trees on the mountain.

'What's that?' Jinx says, spinning round. The rest of us stop and listen.

'I hope it's not Gary and Dean,' Catrin says.

'There!' Tam whisper-shouts, pointing towards a tree further up the slope. On it is a red and green bird, quite big with a long beak. It's gripping the trunk and tapping away.

Catrin smiles. 'Oh, it's a woodpecker!'

'Don't be dull,' Jinx says. 'Woodpeckers aren't real.'

We all stare at him.

'What?' I say.

'Woody Woodpecker! It's just a cartoon character, isn't it?' He does a silly laugh like the cartoon bird and the real one flies off.

'Yeah, there *is* a cartoon character, but woodpeckers are real birds.'

Jinx frowns. 'Are you winding me up?'

'No!' I laugh.

'I thought it was made-up, like the roadrunner.'

'Roadrunners are real birds too,' Tam says.

'No way!' Jinx looks half confused, half impressed.

'Do you know what else is real?' Catrin asks.

'What?'

'*Rabbits*,' she whispers. 'You know, like Bugs Bunny.'

Me and Tam crack up and Jinx turns and storms off, whacking things extra-hard with his stick.

'Aww, don't be like that, mun,' I call after him. 'What's his problem?' I say to Tam. 'He's not normally that bothered if we pull his leg.'

'It's me,' Catrin says. 'I'm his problem.'

'He'll get used to you,' Tam says, jogging after Jinx.

Me and Catrin look at each other. 'Maybe Tam's getting used to you too,' I say.

She shrugs. 'Maybe.'

Jinx says we can stop for our dinner after we've passed the garage at Argoed. He reckons it's a really good picnic spot. There's even a bench. As we go, the river path takes us uphill and the land around us opens out. The mountains don't feel as steep on either side and we can see for miles across fields and farmland.

On our right, at the top of a grassy slope, a huge brown and white bull snorts from behind a gate. Catrin leaves the path.

'Where are you going?' I ask.

'To say hello.'

'You don't say hello to a bull, mun,' Jinx says, but I can tell he's not being mean this time. 'Look at the sign. BULL IN FIELD. It's got a triangle on it – that means danger.'

Catrin huffs. 'I know that. I just want to see it close up.'

'Why?' Jinx and Tam say together.

I shrug. 'She loves animals. She'd be a vegetarian if she didn't like ham so much.'

But as soon as Catrin gets about two feet from it, the bull snorts again, louder this time, and bumps itself against the gate as if it's trying to get at her. Catrin squeals and runs back to us, laughing.

'Girls! Flipping daft, the lot of them.' Jinx shakes his head dramatically and walks on, but Catrin's still laughing.

When we round the bend at Argoed, we have to stop dead because the path is gone. Completely blocked. Looks like there was a landslide. The only way past is by wading in the river, and none of us is going to do that in February!

Jinx gets the map out and we crowd round it. He runs his finger back along his red felt-pen line. He looks up and sucks in air through his teeth like he's a plumber or something.

'There is a way round, one that won't add on much

8

time, but you're not going to like it.'

'What is it?' I say.

'It's through the field we passed back there – the one with Catrin's mate in.'

'Oh heck.'

He means the bull.

CHAPTER TWELVE

NEMO RESIDEO

On the walk back to the field we agree that if the bull is still there, we'll keep going to the viaduct and take Top Road for a while. But that adds nearly two hours so we'd have to eat dinner on the go. Give ourselves the best chance to get a photo before anyone else.

The bull isn't at the gate. Jinx rushes up and climbs on to the bottom bar, leaning into the field. 'I can't see it.'

'Doesn't mean it's not there,' I say.

He turns and sits on the top. 'Jase, it's a bull. I think I'd know if it was there. You saw the size of it – it's not like it'll be hiding in the long grass.'

Me, Tam and Catrin go over to look for ourselves.

'Maybe the farmer took it for a walk,' Tam says, then, seeing our faces. 'To visit the lady cows or something.'

I point to a wooden shelter in the far corner of the field. 'What if it's behind that?'

Catrin leans around me to see. 'Would it fit behind there though? Like, wouldn't its head or its backside be sticking out?'

We're quiet for a few minutes and I know what we're all thinking.

Do we risk it?

'How fast can bulls run?' Tam asks.

'Faster than us, I reckon,' Catrin says.

Jinx straightens his rucksack on his shoulders. 'Dunno, they're pretty big. Can massive things run very fast?'

'I can,' Tam says.

'Fair enough. But if we go back, then it wrecks my whole schedule and that's not good either.'

'So ...' Tam says. 'Wrecked schedule versus probably empty field.' He holds out his hands to show he's weighing things up. 'I say field.'

Jinx and Catrin don't look sure.

'Oh, for God's sake,' I say. 'We're wasting more time standing here talking about it than if we just did it. We could have been on the other side by now! We said we'd only go back to the viaduct if the bull was in the field. And I don't think it is. So let's go.'

I start climbing the gate.

Catrin grabs me. 'No!' She takes a big breath, looking at Tam and Jinx. 'We all go together. Yeah?'

They nod.

We perch on top of the gate, facing the field. I glance at them. They're obviously as petrified as I am, but determined. 'On the count of three. Jump and leg it?'

'Yeah,' Tam says. 'But remember, if someone trips –
Nemo resideo.'

We all look at him like he's gone twp.

'It's Latin. Something my father says. It means
Leave no one behind.'

'Okay,' I say. 'One, two, THREE!'

We jump.

Jinx stumbles as soon as his feet hit the grass, but
he doesn't fall. Tam's halfway across before the rest of
us get up speed. But he keeps looking back, checking
we're all right.

My rucksack slams against my back in an uneven
rhythm. To my right, I can see the look on Catrin's
face, like when we had races at Butlin's last year. She
was never going to win but she was going to give it a
damn good go. A rush of pride comes over me like I
didn't expect when running, terrified, across a bull's
field.

We're over halfway now, the fence on the other
side getting closer and closer. Tam's already on top of
it. Shouting, waving his arms, willing us on.

Then I hear it.

Well, I *feel* it first. The ground rumbling in a way that can't come from three kids' feet. Our heads all turn towards the shed. The bull's coming at us. Fast.

A bizarre sort of strangled wail comes out of Jinx, Catrin gasps, and we all find a new gear from somewhere.

Tam's on the ground inside the field again, holding out his arms, his eyes wider than humanly possible. I daren't look to our left. The bull's thudding hoofs seem to shake the whole field, the whole planet.

I don't need to see it to know it's getting closer.

Jinx reaches the fence first. He starts to climb but Tam grabs him round the middle and launches him over it.

The bull snorts. Catrin screams.

Oh God, oh God, oh God. We're not going to make it. We're not fast enough. We're going to be trampled by a bull. I picture myself thrown high into the air, then I picture it happening to Catrin, and that's worse. I grab her hand and –

And then we're there.

Tam throws Catrin over while I climb.

Me and Tam fall to the ground at the same time, just as the bull slams into the fence. We scramble away on all fours and lie, panting, a bit further up the meadow.

That was close.

CHAPTER THIRTEEN

READY SALTED

We sit in a circle, passing round the last of the bottle of pop. Catrin has some this time.

'It's thirsty work, running for your life,' Tam says.

'We made it though, didn't we?' Jinx grins. 'Look at it now, all annoyed it can't get to us.'

The bull watches from the fence.

'It can't, can it?' Catrin asks. 'Get to us, I mean?

Like, what if it goes back and charges … could it break through the fence?'

'Probably,' I say, putting the empty bottle into my rucksack. 'But I doubt it's bearing a grudge.'

'Oh, I don't know,' Tam says. 'Look at the way it's staring at us, like it's thinking up an evil plan.'

We laugh. But get up very quickly and jog through the meadow, away from the bull. Just in case.

Jinx reckons this detour will add about half an hour so we need to keep moving. He speeds ahead, the bobble on his hat jiggling about.

I glance up at Top Road. Yeah, got to keep moving.

We don't stop till we get to the picnic bench Jinx was on about. We sit on it, all in a row, looking out across the valley to the mountain on the other side. Me and Catrin share our sandwiches with Jinx and Tam. She opens a packet of ready salted, peels off the top layer of bread and puts crisps all over the ham.

'What are you doing?' Jinx asks.

'Improving my sandwich,' she says.

I make a face. 'Spoiling it more like.'

Jinx watches her like she's performing some sort of delicate operation. She puts the top layer back on, pressing it down, and the crisps crunch.

'What's it like?' he asks.

'Try it,' she says, offering him the rest of the packet.

He has a funny look on his face, like he's torn between curiosity and not wanting Catrin to think he likes her. But he takes the crisps and copies what she did.

'Really squash it down,' Catrin says.

He obeys. When his sandwich is ready, he lifts it slowly to his mouth. 'Geronimo!'

I once watched Catrin's baby cousin eat a rusk for the first time. This is a bit like that. Jinx frowns. He chews. He smiles. He nods. He opens his mouth in wonder so we can all see the mushed-up mess inside.

'Aww, this is lush!' He swallows. 'Boys, you have to try this – it's mind-blowing!'

Me and Tam roll our eyes.

Catrin takes another big bite of her sandwich, looking very, very pleased with herself.

CHAPTER FOURTEEN

DIM SIARAD CYMRAEG

Back on the riverside path, Jinx won't shut up about crisp sandwiches. He says, when he gets home, he's going to make a list of everything that might work and do a chart of his results. Be scientific. Then he goes all dreamy-eyed remembering his dinner.

'The way the butter squidges through the broken crisps,' he mutters.

'It's all about the texture,' Catrin says.

He looks at me, shaking his head. 'Jason, you don't know what you're missing, mun.'

We've reached Ystradmawr. It's not that different to Ponty. To our left, across the river, are rows of terraced houses, just like the ones me and Catrin live in. From here it looks like they're stacked on top of each other. A road separates the bottom rows; a bread van drives along it now.

There's also playing fields and a spectator stand. When Ponty Youth played here last year, I stood in there with Dad. We went mad when Tam scored a try – waving our scarves in the air, grabbing each other and jumping up and down. I smile. Sometimes I can do that, remember Mam and Dad and smile because of the good things.

On the right, running along the foot of the mountain is the railway line, then it all slopes up again. There aren't many trains now. Dad told me that, when all the pits were working, the line was really busy but it's not like that any more.

'If we cross over there –' Tam points to a high foot-bridge that spans the river and the road – 'we can check out the papers in that shop, see if there's any news on the Beast.'

'And get more crisps,' Jinx says.

'God, I hope no one's already got a picture,' Catrin says.

'Yep.' Jinx laughs. 'I heard *The Herald*'s also offering a reward for a photo of a rare packet of cheese and onion.'

I clip him round the head. 'Idiot!'

There's one of those boards outside the shop. It's got *Western Mail* written on top. A sheet of paper stuck behind criss-crossed wire says MINERS' STRIKE LATEST – nothing about a wild cat.

'Probably not made the big papers,' Tam says, pushing the door open. 'Let's see if they have any *Herald*s left inside.'

The bell on the door jingles. The shop's smaller than Gwyn's, it's more like a proper paper shop.

Except there's a whole shelf of paraffin lamps and candles. Not cheap either – the owner must be making a fortune. The three-day week isn't tough on everyone.

'Bore da!' says the man behind the counter. 'A sut y gallaf eich helpu heddiw?'

Catrin answers in Welsh. I recognise the words 'dim siarad Cymraeg' and I know she's telling him we can't speak it.

He looks annoyed. This is the thing with the valleys; the further up you go, the Welshier it gets. But it's not our fault we only learn a little bit of Welsh at our school.

'Have you got *The Herald*, please?' Tam asks.

The man looks at him as if he said a load of swear words, but points to a small pile next to the till.

'Oh,' Tam says. 'Yeah … ermm … diolch.'

'Are you being funny?' the man asks. He turns to Catrin. 'Is he being funny?'

'No!' Catrin says quickly. 'He's not. The opposite really. I think he's making an effort.' She glances sideways at Tam, shoos him away and starts talking to the man in Welsh again.

Tam flicks through the paper until the man points out this isn't a library and Tam looks embarrassed and digs into his pocket for 3p.

There's only a quarter of a page about the big cat; a reminder of the reward and the same write-up as before, nothing new. So the good news is no one has beaten us to it. We're still in with a chance.

Me and Jinx are shoving penny sweets into paper bags when the bell jingles again and Gary and Dean walk in.

Flaming hell.

'How come you got here so fast?' Gary asks.

I scrunch up the bag. 'How come you got here so slow?'

They look confused for a second, then Gary says, 'We're on the fastest road, aren't we? No need to hurry – we can take our time, man … go with the flow …' He makes a spaced-out face like he's a hippy or something.

93

'Suits us,' Jinx says, moving closer to Tam. 'We'll find the Beast before you. We've got a plan *and* a schedule.'

Jesus, Jinx, mun, why'd you go and say that?

Dean looks at Gary. 'Oh well, in that case we'll just head back to Ponty then. If this lot have a plan *and* a schedule.'

'I don't want any trouble,' the man says, happy to speak English now.

Dean smirks. 'No trouble. We just want some fags. Ten Benson and Hedges.'

The man serves them, even though they're our age.

Gary turns on his way out of the door. 'Good is it, this plan of yours? Might have to pop off Top Road and check on you from time to time. See how you're getting on, like.'

Back out on the pavement, we quickly shoulder our rucksacks and head off.

'The man said there's been a few in his shop on their way to Blaengarw.' Catrin glances at me. 'But, even if they beat us up there, it doesn't mean they'll find the cat first – or get the best photo. Don't worry.'

But I am worried. Never mind Gary and Dean, there's others after the Beast too. But none of them need the money as much as we do.

CHAPTER FIFTEEN

WET

We decide to walk through Ystradmawr and join the river path further up. Best to keep away from Gary and Dean till they get back on Top Road. The wind whistles between the terraced houses and the sky gets darker. I pull my hood up over my bobble hat and zip my parka right to my chin.

By the time we reach the next bridge it's picking to rain. We jog across, back on to the path where the side of the mountain and the trees give a little bit of cover. Not much though. The rain gets heavier.

'Where's the nearest place to get out of this weather?' I shout, over the wind.

'Hang on,' Jinx says, stopping to pull the map out of the pocket on the side of his bag. We crowd round him, me and Catrin holding the corners of the map so Jinx can find where we are. 'If we go a bit further along – about five minutes if we run – we can go up *this* track to *this* farm.' He puts his finger on to a group of squares and rectangles. 'There might be a barn we can shelter in.'

'*Might be?*' I ask, scrunching my face against the rain.

'Well, if you have any better ideas, let's hear them.'

'Okay, okay, sorry!'

'Let's go,' Tam says, moving to one side. With him out of the way, the wind rushes down the path and whips the map out of our hands. We all reach out to grab it in a mad scramble but it's no use. It spins in the air like a soggy kite and lands in the river.

We watch it float away, Jinx's red felt-pen line still visible until the current drags it under.

'Why didn't you keep hold of it?' he yells.

I point at Tam. 'He said to let go!'

'I said *Let's go*, not *Let go*!'

'God, Jase,' Jinx moans. 'I spent ages on that flipping map! And we *needed* it!'

'It's not my fault,' I say. 'Catrin let go too!'

'Oh thanks, Jason.' She folds her arms. 'Thanks very much.'

'The two of you then!' Jinx shouts. 'You're both idiots!'

'What am I meant to do?' I yell back. 'Go for a swim to fetch it?'

'It's gone!' Tam shouts over us. 'I say we get to the farm. We know where it is and we can make a new plan there.'

So we run. The track isn't far, just like Jinx said. We turn and sprint up the mountain a bit and soon see some farm buildings.

'Looks derelict,' I say.

'That's better,' Tam says. 'No one around.'

We reach a big outbuilding just as the heavens really open. Tam pulls the wooden door closed behind us and we lean against the walls, panting for breath.

We all seem to realise it at the same time. We're still getting wet.

'Christ, mun, there's no roof!' Jinx shouts.

Tam pushes the door back open and we leg it across a yard into a white, brick building. It's got no door but it does have a roof. A few of the slates are missing and it's a bit leaky, but mostly it's dry.

None of us says anything. We just gasp and pant and try to wipe the rain off our clothes. Looks like we're in a stable; it's got little spaces separated by low walls, and hinges where gates used to close off each one. Stalls, I think they're called.

After a few minutes, Tam catches my eye and his mouth twitches. In a brilliant impression of Jinx, he shrieks, *'Christ, mun, there's no roof!'*

We laugh, then Catrin laughs, and then even Jinx

laughs, and I don't know if it's hysteria or what but we can't stop. My stomach is killing and I'm making these weird squeaking noises. Jinx is on the floor wrapped around his bag and Catrin and Tam are leaning over a stall to hold them up.

I haven't laughed like this for a long, long time. It feels brilliant.

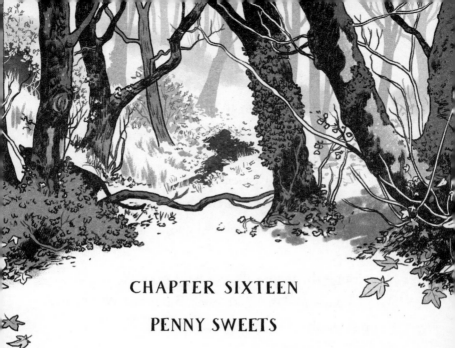

CHAPTER SIXTEEN

PENNY SWEETS

We sit on our rucksacks and try to work out what to do next. Catrin gets the camera and lens out, checking to make sure they didn't get wet.

'Are they okay?' I ask.

She nods. 'The cases kept them dry.' She holds the camera up. 'See? All fine.'

We eat our penny sweets and I look around at my cold, wet friends. We've been chased by a bull, lost the map, our biggest enemies are after the Beast too, and it's still a long way to Blaengarw.

'We can go back if you like,' I say.

They all stare at me.

'I mean, it's not exactly going to plan …' I shuffle on my bag. 'So if you want to cut your losses …'

Jinx nibbles on a stick of liquorice. 'Don't be dull, mun.'

'But – the map – all your hard work …'

'What's up, Jase?' Tam asks. 'You never used to give up so easily.'

Never used to?

I look him straight in the eye. 'Well, maybe I'm not the same as I used to be.'

Catrin and Jinx watch us carefully. They get it, I know they do. But Tam just rummages in his paper bag, not saying anything else.

'Look,' Jinx says, his voice a bit too upbeat. 'I've been thinking about it. As long as we follow the river, we're on the right path. And I reckon other things will come to me on the way. I'll recognise landmarks, or remember what I wrote. The timings will be off but we blew that back at the bull's field anyway.'

Tam looks up. 'We've started now. No one's going back.'

'You sure?' I look at their serious faces. 'All of you?'

'Of course all of us.' Catrin throws a penny shrimp at me. 'I didn't pinch my father's camera for nothing.'

'Wait! What? You *pinched* it?'

She fiddles with the end of her zip. 'Yeah. But it's borrowing really, isn't it? He'll get it back.'

'Catrin, he'll kill you!'

She shrugs. 'He won't. My mother might.' She looks across at me and smiles. 'Doesn't matter though, not if it helps you and Richie.'

Jinx and Tam's mouths are hanging open. They've always had this (false) idea that Catrin is some sort of goody-goody, but that's because they've never wanted to get to know her. And I stopped trying to convince them of how brilliant she is years ago. Not that stealing your father's camera is a good thing, but the reason she did it is.

I smile back at her, wrinkling my nose. 'You're only just out of her bad books after what you said to Mrs Fletcher though.'

'What did she say to Mrs Fletcher?' Tam asks, kind of excited.

'I called her something I shouldn't have, that's all.' Catrin unwraps a chew.

Jinx leans forward. 'What was it?'

'It doesn't matter now.' She puts the chew in her mouth.

He turns to me. 'Do you know what it was?'

'Leave it, yeah?' I say. 'How long till we get to our sleeping point, do you reckon?'

Jinx goes to the stable doorway. The rain's not as bad, but it's dark and murky for four o'clock. 'I made allowances for slight delays so we should still be at the haybarn before sunset. But we can't have any more stops.'

The rest of us get up and I pass Jinx his rucksack. 'And, this haybarn … you're sure there's a roof on it?'

'Funny, Jase. Really funny.'

We pull our hoods up and step out into the gloom.

CHAPTER SEVENTEEN

SKITTLES

It's only drizzling now. We slog back down the track and on to the river path. Behind me and Catrin, Jinx and Tam are trying to guess what she called Mrs Fletcher. I can tell they're loving coming up with worse and worse suggestions.

'They like me better now they think I'm a foul-mouthed thief,' she says quietly.

I glance back at them. 'I think they do.' I nudge

her. 'So do I, to be honest.'

She laughs. 'If I stay friends with you I'll never be allowed out again.'

It's gone five and there's no sign of a farm. Not that we'd see it anyway, it's dark now and our torchlight only reaches so far. We have to pick our way along the path, watching out for tree roots and uneven ground. We all trip at least once. This, and the tiredness, makes us slow. God, I hope we get to the haybarn soon.

I pull my hat down over my ears. 'How much further?' I call to Jinx, who's leading the way.

'Can't be far!' he calls back.

'That's useful.'

'Give him a break,' Tam mutters. 'It's not his fault we lost the map.'

'I know that. I'm just cold and tired.'

'And grumpy.' Catrin glances back, her torch flashing in my eyes. 'But Jinx is right – it can't be far.'

'There!' Jinx stops dead and Catrin bumps into

106

him. We cast our torch beams in the direction Jinx points his. 'Once we get past the fence, we'll have to switch our torches off but it's not far across the field.'

'Why do we have to switch them off?' Tam asks.

'So the farmer doesn't spot us.'

'*What?*' Tam says. 'There are people living there?'

'Yeah,' Jinx says. 'In the house, like, not the barn obviously.'

'Did anyone else think we were staying in an unused barn?' Tam looks at me and Catrin.

We nod.

'Not everywhere is derelict around here, you know,' Jinx says. 'And we'll be fine. Just got to get up early. Now, once we get over the fence, let's turn our torches off and wait a minute for our eyes to adjust, then maybe we need to hold on to each other.' He squints into the distance. 'It's darker than I thought.'

'But this is trespassing!' Tam says, his voice going weirdly high. 'It's against the law!'

Catrin sets off towards the fence. 'Better not get caught then.'

I'm starting to wonder if Catrin's enjoying the rule-breaking a bit too much.

'Look, you two,' Jinx says, following her. 'If you'd rather sleep in the bushes by here, carry on.'

Me and Tam look at each other, shrug, and climb over after them.

There's only one patch of light in the farmhouse, and the flickering means it's coming from candles. I suppose it's the kitchen, it is nearly teatime.

Catrin, Jinx, Tam and me hold on to the straps of each other's rucksacks, like elephants using their trunks to grip the tail of the one in front, and go as fast as we can across the pitch-dark field. I suppose the idea is to keep us together – and it's not a bad one – till Jinx slips and we all go down like skittles. Some of us shout out – I think it's Jinx and Catrin – and we all lie there, a mess of arms and legs and rucksacks. Trying to stay still, teeth gritted, hoping no one at the house heard.

Nothing happens.

'Get off, Tam, mun, you're breaking my ribs,' Jinx moans.

'Shut up,' Tam mutters. 'You're the one who fell.'

'*Shh!*' me and Catrin say together.

We wait about another thirty seconds, then untangle ourselves. Tam leads this time and we move even slower, all checking our footing as we go. My heart's pounding in my head. A short walk has never felt so far.

CHAPTER EIGHTEEN

DARES

The barn is open on one side so we easily slip in, switching our torches back on. It's massive, like about twice the height of my house and full almost to the roof with bales of hay. Must be hundreds – no, thousands – of them in here. All piled up in stacks of different heights. Even this close to the farmhouse, I don't feel too worried about being caught; there are lots of places to hide away.

'I have a question,' Tam says. 'How are we going to cook our hot dogs in a barn full of hay?'

'You're good at campfires and I've got matches and – oh!' I look around. 'I see what you mean.'

'Bit flammable, isn't it?' Catrin says.

'Let's save them for tomorrow.' Jinx waves us round to a space between the bales and the barn wall. 'We've got plenty of non-hazardous grub.'

I'm starving. We sit in a little circle and tuck into the sausage rolls and pasties. The clouds are clearing, so it's easier for us to see by the moonlight streaming in through the open side of the barn. Jinx asks Catrin to show him how the camera works again. I know it's because he wants to have a go with it. She lets him this time and, when the lens comes out with that nice whirring sound, he beams like a toddler with a jack-in-the-box.

Tam lies back on the hay-covered floor and rubs his stomach. 'That was lush, fair play.'

I look at my watch. 'Hey, Jinx, it's half six. Past your bedtime, isn't it?'

He kicks me. 'You're only saying that because you forgot your teddy.'

I laugh. 'True. Seriously though, what shall we do?'

Tam sits back up. 'Fancy a game of Dares?'

We take turns to challenge each other.

Catrin has to put cobwebs round her neck.

Tam runs to a tree and back (which takes about a millisecond).

Jinx eats a mouse dropping (the look on his face is so hilarious Catrin says she wishes she'd taken a photo).

Now it's my turn.

'Climb to the top of there.' Jinx points upwards.

'What? The hay bales?'

'Yeah.'

I stand. 'All right.'

Catrin looks nervous. 'I don't know, Jason. It's really high – and how do you know they're steady?'

'They weigh a ton, these things,' Tam says, patting the bale next to him. 'My father had the boys pulling them in training once. They'll be steady.'

'Solid as a rock,' I say to Catrin. 'Plus, you know I'm a good climber.' She doesn't look convinced. 'Remember down Porthcawl when I climbed that rock face?'

'Yes.' She folds her arms. 'And I didn't like that either.'

'Your face was like this.' I open my eyes and mouth really wide in a shocked expression.

'It's not funny.'

But me, Tam and Jinx think it is.

I look at the bales and rub my hands together. 'Right, where's the best place to start?'

'If you're going to be an idiot, don't expect me to watch.' Catrin takes her bag further into the corner and digs around in it for God knows what.

Tam and Jinx are on their feet now, egging me on. I go over to the other side of the barn, where the path to the top looks easiest, and scramble up two bales at once.

This'll be simple.

CHAPTER NINETEEN

HAY BALES

And it is. The bales are like giant steps that I can pick my way across and up. If one section's too high, I can just go another way. After the fourth one, I stand too far back on a bale and it wobbles. My arms fly out but I lean forward and it all goes steady again. Behind me on the floor, Jinx swears.

'I'm all right!' I whisper-shout.

I climb again. At the top, I walk to the middle and

lift my arms like a champion, grinning down at Tam and Jinx. They mime clapping and whooping, then run around in a circle like nutters.

Catrin appears from her corner.

'See?' I say. 'I did it!'

'Well done.' She doesn't look like she means it. 'Get down then.'

'Oh God, you're such a misery guts sometimes. I'm not going to—'

It's like when you dream you've stepped off a cliff. My head jolts, I leave my stomach somewhere above me and air rushes past my ears. Catrin screams.

It takes forever and one second to land on the floor between two gigantic walls of hay. It's like a damp, narrow, dark, dark tunnel. Except in a tunnel there's a way out.

The others are shouting now, muffled cries on the other side of the thick bales.

I can hardly breathe. The fright and the heavy, stale air stopping my lungs from doing their job. *Get*

a grip, Jason. You're not in much pain, you just need to calm down and think.

But why am I not in much pain? Bouncing off the walls must have slowed me down; I feel scratched and battered but nothing's broken. And there's lots of hay on the floor too, thank God. It broke my fall.

The dust is everywhere … I cough and my eyes stream but I can see some light. Just a little bit. Thin lines which must mean gaps in the wall at one end. The end where my friends are.

It's so hot in here it's hard to believe it's the middle of winter.

'I'm okay!' I try to shout, but the dust catches my throat.

I crawl to the end where the light is. Try again.

'I'm all right!'

'I heard him.' That's Jinx. 'He said he's all right!'

'I am!' More coughing.

Scuffling sounds come from their end.

'I think we can move some bales,' Tam shouts. 'Hang on.'

I'm sweating. I try to breathe into the sleeve of my parka. It helps a bit.

'Jason … are you still there?' That's Catrin.

Of course I'm still here, where the flipping heck does she think I'll be?

'Just get me out!'

Tam makes a noise like that angry bull, and a rectangle of torchlight appears. It gets bigger and bigger as he heaves the hay bale away. Then Jinx's worried face blocks it.

'Get out of the way, you wally!' Tam growls. 'Let him out, mun!'

The difference in temperature hits me like diving into the sea in the middle of summer. Fresh and clear and welcome. Tam reaches in, tucks his hands under my armpits and drags me the rest of the way. I lie on the floor, gasping for air.

Catrin, Tam and Jinx lean over me.

'Jesus Christ, Jase,' Jinx says. 'I bricked it then.'

'Join the club,' I say. Catrin passes me Rhodri's canteen and I sit up to drink.

Suddenly it gets lighter just outside the barn. We all look round. A big figure stands in the doorway with a gas lamp. And a shotgun.

'What the flaming hell's going on in here?'

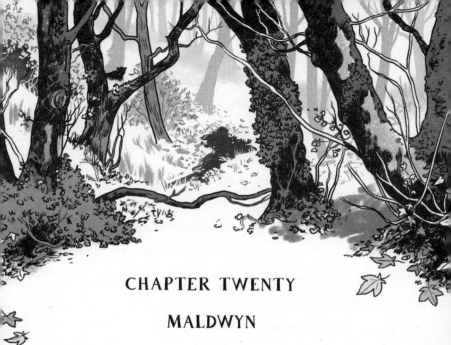

CHAPTER TWENTY

MALDWYN

We sit at the kitchen table, in front of the fire, our hands around steaming mugs of Bovril. The power's on now and the farmer, who says his name's Maldwyn, leans against the kitchen counter, arms folded.

'Flaming daft thing to do,' he says. 'Could have shot you, I could!'

'Take no notice,' his wife says, putting a huge pile

of hot, buttered toast in the middle of the table. 'He's never shot so much as a rabbit.'

'Brenda,' he says. 'I'm trying to teach them a lesson here.'

She laughs. 'By making out you're some mad gunman?'

'All I'm saying is some others in this valley would shoot first, ask questions later – and they'd have a right to. Trespassers can be shot.'

I look up. 'We're sorry.'

'Aye, so you've said.'

'We needed somewhere to stop for the night,' Catrin adds. 'We weren't going to take anything or mess anything up.'

Maldwyn frowns. 'Still doesn't explain why you're here though, does it?'

'We're on our Duke of Edinburgh,' Jinx says.

'A likely story,' Brenda says.

'We are!'

She raises her eyebrows. 'My sister's girl did that and I don't recall her ever having to hide in a barn to get it. *And* –' she plonks a pot of home-made jam on the table – 'I've brought up four boys so I know a lie when I hear one.'

Me, Jinx, Tam and Catrin glance at each other. Tam shrugs, reaching for his second piece of toast.

I take a big breath. 'We're looking for the big cat that people say is in Blaengarw. There's prize money in the paper and, well, we need it.'

Brenda nods and smiles. 'Now, that makes more sense. What do you need it for? Toys, is it? Or sweets?'

My friends all look to me, but I just concentrate on dipping my knife in the jam pot.

Maldwyn watches me and says to Brenda, 'That might not be any of our business, love.'

Jinx and Catrin start to work out how many sherbet dabs they could buy with £100 and I'm glad of the slight change in subject.

Brenda frowns at me. 'I wish you'd let me put some iodine on those scratches.'

The last thing I want is a fuss. 'I'm okay, honestly. Where are your sons now?' I look around as if expecting them to magically appear.

'Pub,' she says. 'Darts match. You'll probably hear them rolling home after. Good boys they are, but they like a drink.'

'Hear them?' Jinx asks. 'You're not kicking us out then?'

'Well,' she says, putting more slices of thick toast on to the plate. 'There's no room in here but you're welcome to the barn. I've got spare blankets you can have.'

'Just don't go climbing my hay bales,' Maldwyn says.

I feel my cheeks burn hot, and not just because of the fire.

Catrin bursts out laughing and we all look at her. 'Just thinking,' she says. 'No room in here. Sleeping in the barn. It's like the Nativity.'

'Yeah, it is!' Jinx says. 'And the way Tam pulled Jason out of the bales – it was like he was being born.' He grins at me. 'Suppose that makes you baby Jesus.'

We all laugh. All except Tam.

'You all right there?' Maldwyn says to him.

'He goes to church,' Jinx says, wiping his eyes. 'He's not allowed to laugh at Jesus.'

Tam grunts and takes another slice of toast.

CHAPTER TWENTY-ONE

OUR RIVER

I don't know if it's those hay bales looming over me, or worrying about Richie, or Jinx's snoring, but I can't sleep. I huff and sit up. When my eyes adjust, I can make out the shape of my three best friends, lying under Brenda's blankets like happy sheep.

Jinx does a massive snorting snore, more like a water buffalo than a sheep. Tam and Catrin don't move. How can they sleep through *that*? I can't stick it any more. I throw off my blanket, wriggle out of my sleeping bag and walk to the yard.

The sky's clear and the light from the moon highlights the outbuildings and trees and roof of the farmhouse. I go over to the fence and lean on it, looking out across the fields. It's very quiet. I can hear the river in the distance.

It's funny to think it's still our river. But it's the same one, the one where Mam took us for picnics on the bank, the one where Dad showed us how to catch bullheads with our hands. We used to put them in a washing-up bowl and watch them swim for a bit before tipping them back into the water.

And it's got our bridge. Me, Tam and Jinx's blue bridge. We do all our best talking there:

About TV;

rugby;

school;

if a humpback whale could fit under the bridge (Tam);

who would win in a fight between a shark and a hippo (Jinx);

and why anyone would think it was a good idea to have coffee-flavoured Revels (me).

We've also done some not-talking there. When bad things happen. We just sit for ages, saying nothing.

That's good too.

And it's the same river me and Richie sat by after the funeral. We had to get away from all the sympathy. We needed it to be just us, because no one else could understand, even the people who said, 'I understand.'

How could they? They weren't us, they'd never had the knock on the door that ripped through our lives, changing everything forever.

'It's just you two now, boys,' they'd said. 'You need to look after each other.'

'Such a shame.'

'There's a pity.'

'Poor dabs.'

'And Jason only twelve.'

'How will you cope?'

'They're at peace now.'

Richie had put his arm around me and walked me out of the house and, without saying anything, we'd sat on the stones down by the river and held each other tight. Sad and terrified and knowing all we had left was each other.

Which is why this trip, this *quest*, is so important. I can't lose my brother too. He can't lose me.

I wipe my eyes and turn back to the barn. Got to try to get some sleep. If the water buffalo will let me.

Even though we set off very early, Maldwyn and his sons are already working in the fields. They wave as we walk down a lane which leads back to the river path. Brenda came to see us first thing, holding out four packages wrapped in foil. 'Bacon rolls,' she'd said. 'Keep you going, they will.'

I'd held mine to my nose and sniffed, wondering if anything in the world smells better than fried bacon.

We eat them about half past ten, but we don't stop.

'These are amazing,' Tam says. 'She even put tomato sauce in them.'

'I know,' Jinx says dreamily. 'That Brenda's a fine woman.'

We crack up, teasing Jinx that he loves Brenda, and he doesn't even mind. Says he'd quite like a nice, jolly wife who makes great food.

Catrin says he's being a male chauvinist pig and why couldn't he make his own bacon rolls and it turns into a whole argument about Women's Lib, which he'll never win because her mother's right into it and Catrin knows everything.

In the end Tam says, 'Just shut up and eat, mun.'

'Yeah,' I say. 'The only pig I'm interested in is the one in this bread roll.'

Catrin pulls out a crispy strip of bacon and looks at it. 'What do big cats eat, again?'

'Anything they can find, I suppose.'

'Oh,' she says slowly. 'I was just thinking about us being animals and eating another animal and then …'

Jinx stares at her. 'I don't think the Beast will *eat us*, Catrin!'

She looks a bit relieved.

He shrugs. 'Just maul us, probably.'

'Take no notice,' Tam says. 'We won't be going anywhere near the cat for it to get us. Anyway, it'll be more scared of us than we are of it.'

I nod. 'Like spiders.'

'You didn't see that one in our bathroom last September,' Catrin says, pulling a face.

'Last *September?*' Tam laughs.

Catrin nods, looking serious. 'You'd remember the day too if you'd seen it. Legs like a carthorse.'

I put a hand on her arm. 'We'll be careful.'

'Oh, that's okay then,' she says, stuffing the last of the bacon roll into her mouth. 'Because that's been going brilliantly so far!'

When we've finished, Tam collects all the foil, scrunches it into a tight ball and puts it in his bag.

'How are we doing for time?' I ask Jinx.

'All right, I think,' he says, brushing crumbs off his

coat. 'We got going early, so that helps. The next big landmark is the old Nant Copperworks. If we're there by half one, we're on schedule.'

'Is that where we went on a trip when we were in Miss Bradford's class?' Tam asks.

'No, that was the Pren Visitor Centre. The bus backfired on the way up that steep hill and Jinx wet his pants,' I say, laughing. 'Remember?'

'I flipping *did not!*' Jinx yells. 'I spilt my squash and you know it.'

I do know it, but it's more fun to pretend I don't.

'Funny squash – what flavour was it? *Pee*napple?'

Tam laughs. 'Weeberry.'

'That doesn't even make sense!' Jinx's voice is getting higher, a sure sign our wind-up is working.

'Weeberry,' I say, slapping Tam on the back. 'You header!'

Jinx pulls his bobble hat down over his ears. 'I didn't wet myself!'

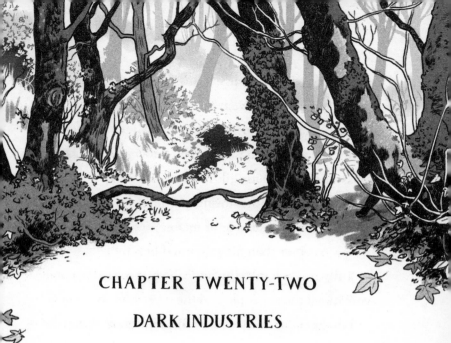

CHAPTER TWENTY-TWO

DARK INDUSTRIES

The Nant Copperworks looks like a rusty funfair from a horror film. It's set behind thick, high railings with spiky tops and, even though the warning signs are everywhere, it's obvious lots of people have got in over the years. There's graffiti all over the place.

We drop our rucksacks and go closer.

There are two brick buildings with tall chimney stacks but no windows, and metal frames where the roofs used to be. Tall platforms and gantries span the yards outside; some have railings, others are like cages. Gigantic wheels, like waterwheels only with teeth like watch cogs, are half underground. There are steps and chain-link fencing and slopes. All red with rust. It's like a drawing of Mars I saw in a book once. If Mars was made of metal.

'It's creepier than I thought it'd be,' Tam says.

I frown. 'It's hard to imagine it when it was working, isn't it? All those people and the noise and the smoke.'

'My grandad says it's all disappearing from the valleys – copper, tin, coal – and it's never coming back,' Catrin says. 'The Dark Industries, that's what he calls them.'

'Did he work here?' Jinx asks.

She looks surprised by the question, but smiles. 'No. At a coal mine in the Rhondda. Still does. When he's not on strike, obviously.'

I wonder where the people go to work now. Wherever it is, they'll only be doing it three days a week. Like Richie. Or they might even be on strike, like Catrin's grandad. Or, worst of all, on the dole. Dad always used to say you can't take work away and not give the people anything to replace it.

I walk away from the others and stick my face between two of the railings to read the graffiti. It's mostly just messy spray paint of people's names and slogans like EAT THE RICH. And a lot of love hearts written in scratchy pen. Catrin appears next to me and nods to one that says Mark loves Angie.

'Richie had a girlfriend called Angie, didn't he?' she says.

'Richie had *loads* of girlfriends.'

But there's no chance of him having one now. Who'd want a boyfriend who was guardian to his little brother? Or who could be going to jail.

'Better keep moving,' I say.

I turn to see Jinx and Tam sitting on their rucksacks, eating midget gems. Jinx holds the paper bag out. 'Fuel. Want some?'

'Erm, do I want some of *my* sweets out of *my* bag?'

He nods, grinning.

I sigh. 'All right, but get up. We can eat on the way.'

There's a shout and two people run at us out of the
bushes. Catrin squeals, Jinx jumps and swears, and
suddenly Gary and Dean are right in front of us. And
Dean's grabbed my rucksack.

'All right, losers? Saw you from Top Road and
thought we'd come and say hello, like. What's in here
then?' He digs around inside my bag.

'Give it here.' I try to grab it but he snatches it
away.

'Ooh, some crisps – bit squashed, aren't they?
Polos, a torch … Oh, and a lovely red sleeping bag,
all rolled up perfect.' He holds it in the air. 'Let's
watch it fly.'

Before we can do anything, Dean steps back
and launches my sleeping bag, like a weird squishy
javelin, over the top of our heads and into the
copperworks.

'Wow,' Gary says. 'Nice throw!'

'That's Jason's!' Jinx says.

'Oh,' Dean says. 'Was it yours, North?' He nudges Gary. 'Was kind of hoping it was Jinxy-boy's.'

'Doesn't matter whose it is.' I glare at him. 'Go and fetch it.'

'Can't, can we?' Dean folds his arms. 'Sign says KEEP OUT.'

Gary nods. 'Yeah. Dangerous, that is. And illegal.'

Catrin marches right up to them, her voice low and kind of threatening. 'Fetch it.'

They laugh in her face.

Jinx joins her. I know him and Catrin must be scared, but here they are, sticking up for me. I look to Tam, who hasn't moved. Again. He could stop this, wouldn't even have to hit them, just look like he would. But no, he only watches.

'Jason needs that,' Jinx says. 'Don't be idiots, mun.'

Gary flinches. 'What did you call us?'

'You heard,' I say.

Dean looks like he's going to lamp me one. I square my shoulders, try not to show that I'm absolutely bricking it.

Tam finally takes a step forward. 'There's no need for any aggro. Just leave it, eh?' He nods to me. 'We'll sort it, Jase.'

I stare at him. 'Oh, *you're* going to go and fetch it, are you? Can't see you fitting under that fence!'

Gary and Dean laugh, slapping each other on the back, all smug because they think they've slowed us down – but I'm not letting that happen.

I take one last look at my sleeping bag, flopped over a gantry, and pick up my rucksack. 'Let's go.' I push past Gary and Dean. 'We've got a reward to win.'

'Dream on,' Gary mutters.

'Jason, wait,' Catrin calls. 'There's a gap down here I can fit through.' She gives Tam a hard stare 'So *I'll* get your sleeping bag.'

She's trying to squeeze between the railings when a yell comes from the other side of the copperworks. 'Oi!'

Everyone's head whips round to see a man in a security guard uniform, coming towards us. A great big bloke, like a marine or something, with a huge dog. And both of them look mean.

'Clear off!' he shouts. 'Or I'll call the police.'

'Go on then,' Gary shouts back. He turns to us, smirking. 'I know his type. All mouth, mun.'

'Sure about that?' Tam says.

'You cheeky little ...' The man starts to run, the dog keeping pace with him, barking and pulling at its lead, straining to get at us.

'LEG IT!'

I don't even know who shouts it, but we grab our rucksacks and run like the wind, splitting off so Gary and Dean head for Top Road, us for the river path. I don't know if it's adrenalin or what, but I'm almost keeping up with Tam. I risk a look back to see the tips of the dog's ears over the top of the long grass.

'Jesus Christ!' I yell. 'He's let it off the lead!'

We make a sharp turn and keep pelting along the path, but it's getting really narrow again, with thick bushes on our right and the river to our left.

Tam stops so suddenly we all bump into each other. He darts up the foot of the mountain, swiping branches out of the way. We follow, because what else can we do? A scrubby little track appears under our feet. Up we go, climbing and climbing, as fast as we can. My chest burns and my heart pounds and I'm about to ask Tam what the hell he's playing at when I see it. A gap in the rocky mountain face. Like a …

'A cave,' Catrin breathes.

We rush upwards, just one last push before my lungs explode. Inside, we flop to the ground, panting and gasping, holding our stomachs and our sides. Even Tam looks wrecked.

CHAPTER TWENTY-THREE

BEANS, BEANS, THEY'RE GOOD FOR YOUR HEART

'We can't go back down there yet and I'm starving,' Tam says. 'Catrin? Fancy helping me make a fire? The twigs in here look dry enough.'

She acts like she hasn't heard him.

'Catrin?' he says again, looking confused. 'What's up with you?'

'What's up with *me*?' She turns on him. 'What's up with *you*, more like! Why didn't you help Jason?'

'*What?*'

'You! You could have forced Gary and Dean to fetch his sleeping bag. But, no, you just had to stand there like a big lemon being all *No need for any aggro*. Well, maybe we needed aggro! Maybe aggro is all they understand!'

Me and Jinx watch them, as though we're hypnotised.

Tam concentrates on building a little wigwam around some scrunched-up paper. 'Like my father says, violence isn't the answer.'

Sometimes I reckon he doesn't have any thoughts that *don't* come from his father, but I'm not getting in the middle of this.

'If you didn't want to hit them, you should have tried to get into the Copperworks,' Catrin rages.

He sighs. 'Even without the giant man and his rabid dog, did you *see* all the danger signs? You know what happened with the bull!'

She shrugs. 'Survived that though, didn't you?'

He says nothing.

'Oh, forget it!' She holds her hand out to Jinx.

'Toilet roll, please. I'm going for a wee.'

He passes it to her and she stamps off into the bushes. Jinx looks to me and does a long, low whistle. He's finally getting to know the real Catrin and I think he's impressed.

Ten minutes later, the smell of warm baked beans fills the cave. Tam hands round spoons and enamel plates, then scoops the beans out.

'Well, this is nice,' Jinx says, like he's an old woman, and the rest of us laugh – even Catrin. Sometimes the funniest thing about Jinx is that he doesn't know he's funny.

When we're all scraping our plates, I sit up and declare, 'Beans, beans, they're good for your heart …' I look around, waiting for them to join in. They all do:

'The more you eat, the more you fart …'

'The more you fart the better you feel …'

'So eat your beans with every meal!'

We say it over and over, getting more and more daft, finding it funnier than it actually is.

Then Tam really does let one go and it echoes

147

round the cave. Jinx asks if he needs paper or stitches, Catrin snorts, and I'm laughing so much I'm in actual pain.

'We need to go,' I splutter.

It takes another five minutes to properly calm down, pack up and get going.

The side of the mountain is so steep we have to grab on to branches as we go. Near the bottom, Jinx slips and tries to turn it into a commando roll but he looks more like a giant, floppy sausage.

Back on the river path, Tam asks, 'How far now, do you reckon?'

'We'll be there before it's dark,' Jinx says. 'And I've had an idea of somewhere better to stay.'

'Where?' I ask.

He taps the side of his nose. 'All you need to know, Jason, my friend, is that there's no hay.'

'Funny guy.'

About half an hour on, something breaks under my foot with a snap and a crunch. It feels weird, and too brittle to be twigs. On the ground, next to some old fencing, is a little pile of broken bones.

'You all right, Jase?' Tam asks.

'Yeah.' I bend down and hold back a patch of ferns. 'Just stood on these.'

He comes for a closer look. 'What are they?'

'Some sort of animal bones. A rabbit or a weasel maybe. Quite small anyway.'

Catrin and Jinx look too. She lifts up the skull, which is still in one piece. 'Look at the fangs on it!'

We pass it round. Tam folds his arms, refusing to touch it. Jinx makes out like he knows all about skeletons and starts to tell us useless facts about bones. Me and Tam pretend to fall asleep and make loud, snoring noises.

'Don't be mean,' Catrin says, but she's giggling.

'*Anyway*,' Jinx says, twyting down to inspect the broken pieces. 'I do know something about bones you'll be interested in.'

'I doubt it,' Tam mumbles, letting out a massive snorty snore.

Jinx ignores him. 'In Llanbryn, some kids found a

human skull in a tree once.'

I open my eyes. 'Serious?'

'Yeah, my grandad told me. It was in the war.'

'What happened?' Tam asks. 'Whose skull was it? Was it a murder?'

Jinx screws his face up. 'I can't remember, but Grandad said it was a really big deal in the village.'

'Fascinating story,' Tam yawns again. 'You should be on *Jackanory*.'

'Well, I'm glad I didn't stand on *human bones*,' I say, doing a big, on-purpose shudder.

Catrin passes the skull back to Jinx. 'Think the Beast could have killed this animal?'

'Nah,' he says. 'We're too far from Blaengarw. But whatever it was wasn't put off by these fangs.' He jigs the skull about near Catrin's face and makes growling noises.

She bats his hand away, giggling again.

'How far *is it*?' I ask. 'In miles.'

'About five, I reckon. We'll get on the right side of the river at the stepping stones – won't be far from there.'

CHAPTER TWENTY-FOUR

STEPPING STONES

'We're meant to cross over *them*?' Tam asks. 'Are you real?'

We stare at the stepping stones. Big, flat-topped rocks stretching across the river from one bank to the other. Big enough to walk on easily – if two of them weren't totally hidden by gushing, crashing water.

'It's like a sodding waterfall!'

145

'Don't be so over the top, mun,' Jinx says. 'It's not that bad.'

'What made you think we could cross here?' I ask, trying not to sound as fed up as I feel.

'They didn't look like this the last time I was here,' Jinx mumbles.

'And when was that?'

Jinx mumbles something else.

Tam cups a hand to his ear and frowns in an over-the-top way. 'Pardon?'

'Last summer, okay?'

'Hmm, last summer.' I scratch my chin. 'Now, let me see … last summer … that'd be the sunniest season, yes? Warmer, with less rain?'

'Stop it, Jason,' Catrin says. 'He didn't know.'

'Didn't know what?' I say. 'That it's winter now?'

'Cut the sarky git act for one minute, will you?' she says. 'We're here now. We need a plan, not another row. Jinx, how far to the next bridge?'

He looks so miserable. 'Too far. Past Blaengarw. We couldn't get there and back before it's dark.'

146

Tam snorts. Catrin gives him a death stare. He lifts his shoulders and mouths, *What?*

She walks off to stand near the first stone.

Jinx goes to the river's edge. 'We could take our shoes and socks off and cross the stones that way.' He looks pathetically hopeful.

'It's too cold and too slippery,' I say.

'You're right! Tam's right! I'm an idiot! A stupid, flaming wally. I didn't think! And now what? I've delayed us and put us in danger because we can't walk in the dark and we can't sleep here and someone else will get a photo before us – hell, Gary and Dean could get a photo before us! And we'll let you and Richie down and it's all my—'

'Whoa!' Tam holds his hands up. 'Calm down, butt!'

'Will you two shut up for a minute?' I say. 'I'm trying to think, mun.'

They shut up, but it doesn't help. I wonder what's worse; walking to the bridge and back in the dark or sleeping out in the open somewhere and setting off early.

147

'Hey,' Jinx says. 'Where's Catrin gone?'

Me and Tam look around. I can't see her anywhere.

'Catrin!' I shout.

'I'm over here!' she calls back. 'I remembered passing this, but I need some help. Tam – get over here.'

What's she on about? Passing what?

Further down the path, she's holding up one end of a plank of wood. It's from the old fencing.

'Genius,' Jinx whispers.

CHAPTER TWENTY-FIVE

SLOW AND STEADY

Jinx and Catrin stand by the water's edge. They point at the stones, lift the plank, put it down again, talk fast. They've told me and Tam to go away so they can concentrate.

'What's the plank for, d'you reckon?' Tam asks.

I shrug. 'Sailing across?'

He screws his face up. 'Ooh, don't let Catrin hear you being sarky again.'

She waves us over. The plank's balanced between two big stones, about five inches from the ground.

'Stand on that,' she says to Tam.

'Erm … okay.'

'Now bounce a bit,' Jinx says.

Tam bends his knees and jigs up and down. The plank flexes but doesn't creak or crack.

Jinx looks at Catrin. 'It'll work.'

She nods. 'If it holds Tam's weight, it'll easily hold ours.'

I look across the river. 'Are we doing what I think we're doing?'

'Yep.' Catrin beams. 'DIY portable bridge.'

'A Jenkins and Rees patented design.' Jinx beams back at her.

Tam looks at me, eyebrows raised. 'Can't be worse than running from a bull … can it?'

I look at the water tumbling and foaming at the places where the river covers the stones.

Can't it?

'This is what we do,' Catrin says. 'It's the eighth

and tenth stones which are underwater so Tam will carry the plank to the seventh – is that okay, Tam?'

'Yep.'

'We'll follow one by one. Tam will use the plank to get across the first gap then wait on the ninth stone – the middle one. The next person will join him and the plank will go over the next gap so they can cross to the other side.' She nods to Jinx.

He nods back. 'Tam, you stay on the middle stone, passing the plank back and forth till we're all past the gaps. The tricky bit will be sharing the middle stone – especially with you – so we'll have to hold on to each other.'

Tam shrugs. 'Fine by me.'

'It'll work,' Catrin says. 'We just have to go slow and steady. Then we'll be fine.'

God, I hope she's right.

We stand, one behind the other, on the first four stones; Tam, then Catrin, then Jinx, then me.

'Ready?' she calls.

'Ready!' we answer. But I'm not sure I am. Where

151

we need to use the plank is the fastest, deepest part of the river. We could get dragged under or swept away. I love this river, but I don't want to die in it.

Catrin smiles at me, and she's so sure, so determined, that I reckon I must be wrong. We'll be fine. Like she said.

Tam moves on to the next stone and Catrin steps on to the one he just left. When Tam reaches the fourth stone, he looks back. We're all off ground now. He gives us the thumbs-up and we answer in the same way.

We all move one more stone in.

With the water whooshing below me and a bulky rucksack on my back, I have to concentrate hard on my balance. How Tam's managing it holding a thick plank I have no idea.

Go slow and steady, Catrin said. *Then we'll be fine*.

I don't feel fine.

Tam reaches stone number seven, puts the plank down and slides it on to the one after the gap. He presses down on it.

'How's it feel?' Jinx calls over the river's din.

Tam doesn't look up, just lifts his thumb again.

One step on the plank and he's on the middle stone. Now it's Catrin's turn. He moves the plank first, then stays twtying down as she steps across to join him. He moves the plank again and gets up. They're really close, they have to put their arms around each other to balance. They look like they're doing one of those slow dances teenagers do at the end of a disco, as they gradually turn till she can step on to the plank.

Two more stones and she's across!

Tam moves the plank and it's Jinx's turn next. Their slow dance would be funny if it wasn't so scary out here.

I make my way across the stones. It's horrible because I have to look down to make sure of where I'm putting my feet, but the water rushing past makes my head feel thick and fuzzy, like it's full of cotton wool.

Deep breaths. One steady step at a time.

On the seventh stone, I look up to see Jinx joining Catrin on the bank.

'It's not too bad, Jase,' he calls. 'Just watch that one there.' He points. 'Second from the end, it's really uneven.'

I nod, unable to shout back. My mouth's too dry.

'All right?' Tam's waiting for me to step on the plank.

But I can't make my foot move.

'Trust me,' he says. 'I'm an expert now.'

But it's not him I don't trust, it's this wet plank, this rushing water. Myself.

It's like the river's sucking me downwards; the loud shush pours into my ears, whirls inside my head, making me dizzy – *No, Jason! Deep breath!*

Don't …

Get …

Dizzy!

Tam's holding out his hand and I take it. I feel better, calmer.

Three, two, one.

I put my foot on the plank and step to the middle

154

stone. Tam's never seemed so big. He moves the plank, straightens up and we do our shuffly dance. Now I'm here I can't believe this is working. It's so rickety, so dangerous. And the next stone looks craggier than the others.

Tam smiles. 'Nearly there.'

I don't move.

'Come on, Jase,' Jinx calls. 'You've done the worst bit.'

I look down at the plank. *Have I?*

Tam speaks so only I can hear him. 'You know I'd never let you fall, don't you?'

We stare at each other for a few seconds, which is really weird standing so close on this stone. I nod.

He scrunches his face up. 'Did that sound soft?'

'A bit, yeah.'

But it's what I needed.

Plank.

Stone.

Stone.

Riverbank!

My legs feel wobbly like stepping off a boat. Tam doesn't waste any time, and soon we're all standing on the pebbles watching the river.

'I can't believe that worked,' Catrin says.

'What?' I say. 'But you were all, *Slow and steady, we'll be fine.*'

She smiles. 'Had to be, didn't I?'

CHAPTER TWENTY-SIX

A HUMAN TREE TRUNK

About ten minutes up the path, a dog bounds towards us out of nowhere. It's huge and, at first, I think it's the one from the copperworks but it isn't. Thank God! It's a German shepherd, all long hair and giant paws.

'Prince!' A man comes round the corner. He sees us and waves a dog lead in the air. 'Sorry, boys – oh – and girl.' He grins. 'He's friendly, honest! Just excited.

Loves the river, he does.'

Prince bounds back to his owner, who tells him to sit and the dog does it straight away.

'Can I stroke him?' Jinx asks.

'Yeah. He doesn't bite.'

Tam looks like he doesn't believe it. The man laughs. 'Thought he was the Beast of Blaengarw, did you?'

'It's not funny,' Tam mutters under his breath. 'Animal should be on a sodding lead.'

'You know about the Beast then?' Jinx rubs Prince's thick chest coat.

'Everyone does round here, don't they?' He clocks our rucksacks and bedrolls. 'You camping?'

I nod.

'Funny time of year to do it.'

'It's for our Duke of Edinburgh award.'

Jinx gives me a sneaky thumbs-up.

The man watches Catrin play with his dog. 'Not looking for the Beast then?'

Jinx tries to sound casual. 'Don't really know

much about it, to be honest.'

'No?' He looks pleased to be able to tell his story. 'Well, last night some blokes were talking about it down The Colliers – that's my local – the landlord's brother's got a few chickens up Blaengarw way. Well, he did have. Something was getting them – thought it was a fox. But he stayed up one night with a Thermos and a shotgun and – damn him if it wasn't a gigantic cat! Scared the living daylights out of him. Fell backwards, fired a shot into the air and scared the bugger off.' He glances at Catrin. 'Oh, pardon my French.'

'It's all right,' Jinx says. 'She's said worse.'

I elbow him. 'So, it was killing chickens?'

'Yeah, should have known it wasn't a fox because it was taking them away. They found fully stripped carcasses on the field. Foxes don't do that. They kill for fun, they do.' He taps his thighs and whistles. Prince runs back to him.

'Some people think it's a myth,' Catrin says. 'The Beast.'

'Nah, must be true, mustn't it?' He strokes the dog between his massive, fluffy ears. 'Why would he lie?'

By the time we get to Craigwern we're gasping for a drink, so we leave the path for Tam and Catrin to go into the VG store. They're taking ages. It's raining again, so me and Jinx wait in the bus shelter across the road; he's got a new stick which he taps on the pavement, humming the *Trumpton* theme tune quietly to himself.

He pulls out his penknife and starts whittling the end of his stick. He reckons he can make it into the shape of a duck's head. I don't know where he gets these ideas from. Mam always used to say he was *a unique boy*, which I reckon is mother-code for 'weirdo'. A picture of her, standing in the kitchen, listening to him going on about his latest daft scheme, fills my mind. She's laughing and making us jam sandwiches. She had a great laugh. I hope I never forget what it sounded like.

'They only had pretend cola, not the good stuff, so

we got these.' Tam's on his way across the road, holding up two cans of pop. Catrin follows with another two. All together they've got an R. White's lemonade, two Shandy Bass and a Tizer. Lush.

They step into the shelter and pull their hoods down.

'What took you so long?' I ask.

'Seeing if anyone knew anything else about the Beast,' she says.

'If you keep doing that, everyone's going to know we're not on our Duke of Edinburgh!'

Tam hands me the Tizer. 'Jase, mun, they know that anyway! Four kids suddenly camping – on their own – when there's a reward going. There's no point pretending, is there? People up here don't know us and I'm sure Prince's owner guessed, and he wasn't bothered.'

'And,' Catrin says. 'Look at us – we're hardly the Duke of Edinburgh types. It's only swots who do that.'

Jinx looks as if he's trying to work something out. 'I thought you were a swot?'

'It's not me who's obsessed with library books and maps, is it?' She pulls her hood back up. 'Come on, the rain's not so bad now.'

We have to walk in single file over the stone bridge as it's one for cars and the pavement is really narrow. At the end is a road sign. *Blaengarw 3 miles.* We go down a slope to get back to the river.

Three miles. Not far now.

'I can smell chips!' Tam says, turning his head and sniffing the air like a bloodhound.

'Ooh, me too,' Catrin says. 'I think someone's down by the river with them. Must have got them from the Craigwern chippy.'

Jinx pouts. 'We should've got some.'

The amazing smell of salt and vinegar gets stronger and voices reach us over the rushing of the water. Two lads are sheltering under a tree on the riverbank, stuffing sausage-in-batter into their faces like pigs.

Gary and Dean.

'Oh, not again,' Catrin moans quietly.

I look at the branches above them. Raising a finger to my lips, I wave my other hand at my friends to get them to move back. They do, but Catrin frowns, mouthing, *What are you doing?*

You'll see, I mouth back with a wink.

I creep closer to Gary and Dean, then reach up and grab a big branch with both hands. I slowly pull it down as far as I can, then let it go with a whipping whoosh. Raindrops ping off, showering the boys.

They leap up, half-chewed chips and filthy swear words flying from their mouths.

Me, Tam, Catrin and Jinx leg it along the path, laughing our heads off.

We don't slow down till we're sure Gary and Dean are far behind.

Jinx claps me on the back. 'Jason North, that was a *classic!*'

'Teach them to chuck my sleeping bag, won't it?' I say, grinning.

'They must be soaking,' Catrin says, taking off her bobble hat and smoothing down her hair.

'Looks like they meant what they said too – about taking their time.'

'Good job they're idiots as well as total gits,' Jinx says. 'Trouble is, Gary's brother's not so thick, is he? I still can't believe Richie's tangled up with Snook. I mean, I know he had no choice but …'

'He did have a choice though,' Tam says.

I stare at him.

'There's other ways to get money.' He shrugs. Actually shrugs.

What?

'Not all crimes are committed for money,' Jinx says. 'Some do it because they're nutters.'

'Richie's not a nutter,' Catrin says.

'I know *that*,' Jinx goes on. 'But this bloke down Sandways attacked his next-door neighbour over an argument about trees – smashed all his neighbour's garden gnomes first, then tried to lasso him with a hosepipe. Nutter. I mean, it all *sounds* funny but—'

'Will you shut up about flaming garden gnomes and hosepipes?' I shout, jerking my hand towards

Tam so that Tizer froths out over my fingers. 'I want to know what *he* means.'

Tam looks at me, eyebrows raised. 'What? I'm just saying, prisons are full of people who've done things for the money.'

'What's that supposed to mean?'

'It means …' he says, pausing like a teacher who wants to make a point, and I feel my blood start to boil, 'that there are good people who do bad things. But they can't expect to break the law and get away with it.'

'Oh, here we go,' I say. 'Here comes the lesson from Mr Follow-the-Rules-Never-Does-a-Sodding-Thing-Wrong.'

A look flashes across his face. Sort of hurt and confused, but right now, I really don't care.

'Are you saying Richie deserves to go to prison? Is that what you're saying?'

Tam stops and folds his arms. They look massive like that and, for just a split second, I wonder why I'm picking a fight with him, but I can't help myself.

'Do you think I'd be here if I wanted that to happen?'

Now he's being reasonable and I can't stand it. So I drop my can and push him. Hard. Hard enough to floor most thirteen-year-old boys. But Tam's not like most thirteen-year-old boys. He's a human tree trunk.

'Steady,' he says, and he says it so calmly that I want to smack him one. Right in the face.

'Yeah, Jase, leave it,' Jinx says, hopping about on his feet like he doesn't know what to do.

Catrin does though. She steps in between me and Tam, facing me. *Walk away*, she mouths.

And I do. Because the look in her eye tells me I'm on the edge of something I'll regret forever.

CHAPTER TWENTY-SEVEN

WHEN THE LID BLEW OFF

I've done it before. Lost it. Completely and totally lost it. Catrin was there. And I know it frightened her.

When someone you love dies, you expect to cry. When two people you love die at the same time, you imagine you'd never stop. But I couldn't cry at all. Not for weeks. People – relatives – friends – nosy sods who barely knew us but wanted to get involved – had

sat at our kitchen table, or on our settee, and wiped
their eyes. At the funeral, so many were at it, I reckon
Gwyn must have sold out of tissues.

But not me.

Which gave them more to talk about. I heard them
at the wake, in the street, down the shops.

'Aww God help, he's in shock.'

'It's a worry though.'

'Cold, I call it. Not crying when your parents have
died.'

'Perhaps there's something wrong with him.'

And it was like everything they said – the kind
things and the mean things – all added to the weight
pressing down on me. Because no one tells you that
grief will be heavy. Actually physically heavy. It was as
if my bones were made of lead. It was an effort to exist.

And the heaviness pressed down but the anger and
pain bubbled up, like a pressure cooker. Catrin was
with me when the lid blew off.

We were in my bedroom. Aunty Pearl was down
the Co-op, but she'd asked me to sort out anything I

had for the jumble sale the Scouts were doing. Catrin said we could tidy my room at the same time and I thought we might as well. She was sorting my *Beano* annuals into date order – she loves doing things like that too – when I found them.

Cards from my twelfth birthday. My stomach flipped and my mouth went dry because I knew, somewhere in that pile was the card from Mam and Dad. The last one I'd ever get.

My heart thudded in my ears.

I found it.

It had Snoopy and Woodstock on the front. It said *Happy Birthday* and Mam had stuck one of those little stickers on that she liked to buy from Gwyn's. See-through, with gold swirly edging. In the middle, it said *Son*.

One word. Three letters.

That's when it hit me. I wasn't anyone's son any more. I was just Jason North. The Ponty Orphan.

I didn't read it, just put it carefully in my desk drawer. And then it started. The pain and anger

169

bubbled slowly at first, and I ripped all the other cards to shreds. Catrin didn't even notice that. The bubbles swirled till it felt like there was a whirlpool inside me. It grew, churning and spinning. And the only way to let it out was to unleash chaos. Catrin looked up and, all of a sudden, I couldn't stop.

And I didn't care.

I grabbed anything I could lay my hands on. The bits of birthday card, the pile of too-small clothes for the jumble, my alarm clock. I chucked them in all directions. I tore out drawers and smashed them against the wall. I hurled my pillow on the floor but it just flumped. No good. I needed things to clatter and smash and break.

Catrin was screaming at me to stop, tears streaming down her face. But I couldn't – didn't want to. Toys hit my desk. My lamp went flying. I picked up my chair, swung it around and that's when I heard the crack and the whimper.

Catrin was holding the side of her head. Blood trickled down her cheek.

Jesus Jesus Jesus. What had I done?

I dropped the chair and grabbed her arm, leading her to the bed where she thumped down, shaking.

I managed to pull her hand away and saw a small but deep gash near her left eye. I felt sick.

'I'm sorry,' I kept saying, over and over again.

'Just get something to stop the blood,' she said, breathing fast.

I ran to the bathroom, grabbed a flannel and wet it. I wrung out as much water as I could, then ran back.

I wiped her cheek, then Catrin took the flannel and pressed it to the cut. I knelt on the floor in front of her, panting hard. Feeling ashamed.

When the blood stopped, she put the flannel on her lap and looked at me.

'I'm so sorry,' I said again.

But she took my hand and I remember it being cold and wet from the flannel and she looked right at me and she said, 'It doesn't matter. None of it matters.'

And that's when I finally cried, and Catrin cried with me.

We tidied up, hid the broken things deep in the dustbin. She told her parents that she fell and hit her head. She didn't tell anyone and we never spoke about it again.

But I know it's on her mind now.

CHAPTER TWENTY-EIGHT

SAYING SOMETHING

They leave me alone. Let me walk ahead to deal with my own thoughts my own way. By the time I calm down I feel exhausted and a little bit stupid. What was I thinking, squaring up to Tam like that?

When we get to a part of the river where the bank is wide, Jinx says it's a good chance for a rest. I think he only says it because he's fed up of walking along under the big black cloud of my mood. We go down the slope to the pebbles; it's like our place under the Blue Bridge. I wander as far as I can and sit down on a big stone.

I pull my hood up and, after a minute, feel someone coming closer.

Tam sits next to me and nods towards Catrin and Jinx. Looks like they're playing Poohsticks off the bank. 'He'll never grow up, will he?'

I don't answer. He's not getting off the hook that easily.

He takes a really deep breath, head down, scratching lines on a stone with a smaller stone. 'You must know I don't want Richie to go to prison.'

'Must I?'

He sighs. 'I keep getting it wrong, don't I?'

I look out across the water. 'Yep.'

Silence.

After a couple of minutes, Tam breaks it. 'Shall I leave you alone?'

No, Tam. Because that's what you want, isn't it? To

174

go off and pretend like nothing happened. Well, not again. Not this time.

'How come you can have all these opinions about my brother but you never even *mention* my parents?'

He does this odd little jolt, goes stiff and blinks.

I turn my head and stare right at him – like it's a dare – but he won't look at me. The scratched stone suddenly goes dark in one place. Like something dripped on it.

Jesus, he's crying.

I didn't think Tam had tear ducts. Someone broke his leg in a really dirty tackle once, and I swear the crack echoed all round Ponty. But he never even sniffed.

'I'm sorry, Jase. I'm really sorry. I don't know what to say. About your mam and dad. I *never* know what to say.'

'So you say nothing.'

I tug at his hood and his head jerks up. I want him to see my face when I tell him how rubbish he's been since they died. How he's let me down. How even

175

Jinx has handled it better. But something stops me, maybe it's the look in his eyes.

'I'm scared of upsetting you,' he says. 'Of making it worse.'

I zip my hood tighter. A wind's getting up. 'Do you know what?'

He looks at me, all worried and hopeful at the same time.

'Not talking to me, changing the subject every time my parents or the crash are mentioned, *that's* what makes it worse, Tam.'

'I'm sorry,' he says again.

But I think I get it now. He doesn't really, *really* know me like Catrin does, and he's not as upfront as Jinx. Sometimes it must be hard for him too – for all of them – being best mates with *the Ponty Orphan*.

'It's okay.'

He half smiles.

'I mean – it's not okay,' I say. 'It's been flipping awful – and you've been a right wally. But ... well ... we're mates, aren't we?'

He puts his arm round my shoulders and squeezes it for about a millisecond. 'Want a Toffo? I got them in the VG because you like them.'

I take one. 'Thanks.'

'Could have had one earlier if you hadn't done your Muhammad Ali act.'

I peel off the wrapper and pop the chew in my mouth. 'Never seen Ali push anyone.'

He laughs. 'Fair play.'

And I know we're all right again.

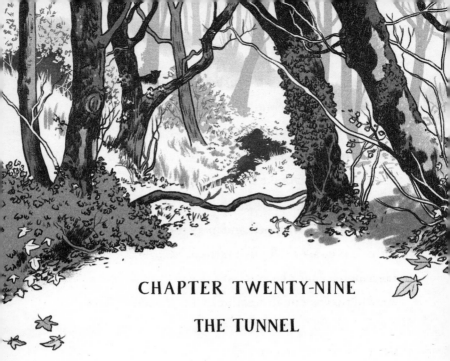

CHAPTER TWENTY-NINE

THE TUNNEL

Catrin and Jinx walk together, further up the path, giggling and quarrelling over whose Poohstick was whose, like they've been friends their whole lives. I glance sideways at Tam. I thought this trip – this quest – was about fixing things for me and Richie, but maybe it's about other things too. I smile to myself, because I'm starting to feel something I haven't felt in a long, long time. I think it might be hope.

Suddenly Tam ducks, clutching the side of his head. 'Whoa! What the … ? Did you see that? Something just missed me!'

Catrin and Jinx spin round.

She frowns. 'What's the matter?'

'Did you see it, Jase?' Tam asks.

'Something flew past us, yeah. Couldn't be a bird, could it? I mean – Oww!' I rub the back of my leg. 'It got me then!'

Catrin twties down and picks up a stone. 'This bounced off you.'

We look around nervously.

Then it really starts.

Lots and lots of stones – small rocks really – rain down on us from both sides, stinging, hurting, cutting.

'AMBUSH!'

'Look at them run!'

Gary and Dean laugh like the maniacs they are as they pelt us.

None of us dares look back in case we get one in

the face. Thank God for our rucksacks, they take the brunt of it.

'Do this!' Catrin yells, wrapping her arms over the top of her bobble hat. 'Protect your heads!'

We do it, following the curve of the river as we run. They're still after us, but there aren't so many stones now; they must be stopping to gather more ammo on the way.

'Here!' Jinx shouts. He turns right, into some sort of tunnel. We follow and he glances back, over our heads. 'I don't think they've seen us. Torches on, we're going this way.'

Four clicks later and four beams of light lead us down the tunnel. It's all lined with bricks, like a creepy cellar, and the roof curves over us. There's puddles and bits of rubble and sticks on the ground. And gaps in the brickwork. God, I hope it's not going to cave in.

'I can't see the end,' I say. 'It must be really long.'

'About half a mile,' Jinx says. 'It's one of the old mine tunnels. It cuts through the side of the mountain and comes out further up the valley. Come on!'

'How does he know these things?' Catrin asks, as me, her and Tam jog after him.

'Haven't you learned by now?' I nudge her. 'Jinx knows loads of useless – I mean interesting – facts.'

He shouts over his shoulder, 'If I didn't, you lot wouldn't last five minutes and you know it. My role in this quest is *vital*.'

Fair enough.

We jog along, the torchlight cutting through the darkness like we're in a cartoon. If we thought it was dark in the blackouts, it's nothing compared to this. It's a blackness I've never known before. It's like it's not made of air.

And it's so cold; a creeping, damp sort of cold, like being deep, deep in a cave.

'Shh!' Tam grabs my arm. 'Listen.'

We freeze. Muffled noises come from somewhere behind us.

'Could be rats,' Catrin says.

'Not unless rats can swear,' I say.

'Run!'

The tunnel curves to the left and, straight away, we see an arch of light. The way out! We speed along, leaping over bricks and branches, torch beams flying all over the place. Gary and Dean must hear us because they start to shout.

The exit is different to the entrance, it's got a gate which covers the very top, a bit like a portcullis on a castle. As we pass under it, Tam has to duck. They all keep going but I stop to look at the gate. It's rusty and must have gone up and down by a winding mechanism – there's a set of cogs and a handle.

'Hey!' I point to the portcullis. 'Reckon we can get this closed?'

'Oh!' Catrin says. 'Yes! Block them in!'

I grin. 'Tam? Want to put some muscle into it?'

Tam dumps his rucksack on the ground, grips the handle and pushes. It moves a bit, then sticks.

'Need help?' I say.

He shakes his head. 'I can … do … this …'

Catrin looks down the tunnel. 'Torches! They're coming!'

Tam goes harder, like he's Hercules or something.

I don't know which groans the loudest, the mechanism or Tam, but it's shifting. The portcullis starts to grind down with a shuddering squeal that echoes through the tunnel.

'They're running!' Catrin's bouncing on her feet now.

'Come on, Tam!' Jinx shouts.

Gary and Dean speed up, but they aren't going to make it. The portcullis clatters into the ground with an almighty clang. They smash into it, swearing and yelling. They try to pull it up, but it's no use.

'You wait,' Dean roars. 'I'm going to smash your stupid heads in. ALL OF YOU!'

'Yeah, right.' Jinx cocks his head towards Tam. 'As if you could beat *him*.'

'Ahh, big man on the other side of this gate, aren't you, Jinxy-boy?' Gary says. 'Well, you won't be so mouthy with your teeth rammed down your throat!'

183

I'm sick of this, sick of them picking on the easiest target. Jinx would do anything for me and it's time I paid him back. I step closer to the bars. 'Touch him and you'll have me to deal with.'

And I mean it. I really do. Even if this gate wasn't between us, I'd still front up.

Gary must see the crazy rage in my eyes because he looks away first.

'Let's go,' I say.

I turn, and my friends follow me along the path.

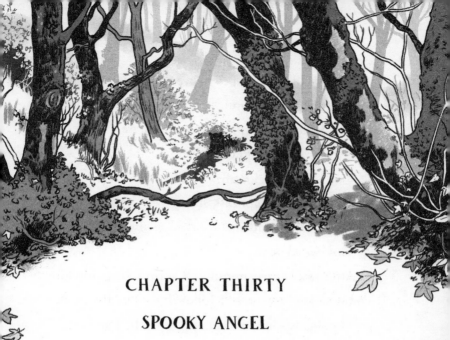

CHAPTER THIRTY

SPOOKY ANGEL

Jinx catches up with me and nudges my arm. Really quietly, he says, 'Thanks Jase.'

I glance at him and smile. 'It's all right.'

He jogs ahead and turns to face us all, walking backwards. 'Let's have a singsong, is it?' He waves his arms like a conductor. 'Oh, you'll never get to heaven …'

Tam and me look at each other, and join in.

'Oh, you'll never get to heaven …'

'In a baked bean tin.'

'In a baked bean tin.'

Catrin's singing now too.

'Cos a baked bean tin's …'

'Cos a baked bean tin's …'

'Got baked beans in.'

'Got baked beans in.'

After about five minutes, Catrin whispers, 'How come he knows so many verses?'

'He makes some of them up himself,' I say.

'Thought I hadn't heard that one about nuns before.'

We join in again.

'Oh, you'll never get to heaven …'

'Oh, you'll never get to heaven …'

'In Jason's pants.'

'In Jason's pants.'

'Cos Jason's pants …'

'Cos Jason's pants …'

'Are full of ants.'

'Are full of ants.'

And on we go …

BLAENGARW

It's only a little sign, but it feels good to see it here, at the side of the road. It's like we achieved something just by getting this far. The low sun's shining on it, lighting it up like a welcome. Blaengarw is small, much smaller than Ponty. Maybe fifteen streets, a shop and a pub. In the distance, a church steeple sticks up behind some trees.

'Better try to find out exactly where the cat's been sighted,' Catrin says. 'There's a lot of fields around here. Could be any of them. I'll nip in the shop.' She plonks her rucksack on the pavement. 'Watch this for me a minute.'

We wait outside, dumping our empty cans and other rubbish in the bin. It's getting dark quickly. A minute ago, I could easily see the end of the road, now it's shadowy.

When Catrin comes back out, she's smiling. 'The woman was nice and friendly – and said quite a few people have been up here looking for the Beast, but no one's claimed the money, yet.'

'That's good,' I say.

'Yeah, anyway, the place where people reckon they've seen it is a few miles up there. She told me which way we need to go.'

'A few miles?' Tam groans.

'Yeah, turns out it's the Beast of *Near* Blaengarw.' Catrin wrinkles her nose. 'But that's okay, isn't it? We can sleep, set off early again and be there first thing.'

I look up the road. 'If it's only a few miles, why don't we walk it now? Find some shelter in the field, camp there, save more time?'

'It'll be pitch dark soon,' she says gently. 'We can't risk getting lost. And we can go faster in the morning, after we've had a rest. My legs are aching.'

'I suppose.' I sigh and turn to Jinx. 'Where *are* we sleeping?'

'Not far,' he says. 'I can see it from here.'

But he won't say exactly where or what it is. Even after everything, I sometimes think this is a bit of a game to him and Tam; an adventure. They don't really understand what's at stake for me and Richie.

'Early though, eh?' I say. Now we're this close, it feels almost painful to have to wait. 'Like, as soon as there's enough light. Promise?'

'Promise,' Catrin says, and the boys nod.

As we walk, fuzzy light from candles and lamps starts to flicker through the net curtains in the windows of the houses.

'I wonder when all this will end,' Tam says. 'The power cuts. The strike.'

'My dad says he can't see the miners backing down,' Jinx says. 'So the Prime Minister will have to.'

Catrin pulls her scarf tighter. 'I hope it's soon. My parents are starting to worry about money. They try to keep me and Rhodri out of it, but I know Dad hates working less hours.'

'You'd think people would be happy not to have to

go to work every day,' Jinx says. 'You know, if they didn't need the money.'

'Everyone needs the money round here though,' I say.

At the end of the road, Jinx stops. 'Oh! Must be up here.' He points to a narrow pathway between a house and a boarded-up electrical repair shop.

Tam frowns. 'Up there?'

'Yep.' Jinx strides off and we follow him, giving each other questioning looks.

The pathway leads to a gravel track which runs around the back of the houses and up the mountain. *Where the heck is he taking us now?*

We dig out our torches and tramp on. It can't be a house, Jinx would have said if we were staying with someone he knows. A hostel? No, we don't have money for that.

The hedges on either side of the track get higher, blocking our view.

'Come on, Jinx, mun,' Tam says. 'It's turning into the middle of nowhere. Give us a clue, will you?'

'Can't be far now,' Jinx mutters. 'Wait … you'll see. It'll be good.'

The path curves round and suddenly there aren't any hedges any more but there is a low, stone wall surrounding …

Catrin blinks. 'You're kidding me!'

It's a graveyard. The church in the middle of it must be the one we could see from further down the village. But it's dark – no candlelight flickers inside.

'It's a church!' Tam says.

'Well done,' Jinx says, clapping. 'Nothing gets past you, does it?'

'Shut it, Jenkins. I am *not* sleeping in a church!'

'Huh? I thought you'd like it more than any of us.'

'It's blasphemous!'

'What's blasphemous about it though?' I ask. 'You go to church every Sunday.'

'To *worship*, not to trespass.' He stares up at the steeple. 'Again.'

The clouds drift away and moonlight picks out a

huge, stone angel. Why do people want creepy statues watching over their loved ones?

Catrin's looking thoughtful. 'They don't lock churches, do they?'

Tam shakes his head.

'Then everyone's welcome. How can that be trespassing?'

'Yeah!' Jinx says. 'And wouldn't God want you to be safe?'

Tam folds his arms. 'Now you're twisting things.'

I sigh. 'It's only blasphemy if you believe in God, and I don't – so I'm doing it!'

Catrin and Jinx follow me into the graveyard. At the porch, we turn back.

'Look,' I call to Tam. 'It's either sleep in the church with us, or out here with the spooky angel.'

Tam grabs his rucksack and stomps towards us, grumbling about whatever happened to *Nemo resideo*.

CHAPTER THIRTY-ONE

NOT A SÉANCE

I push open the big wooden door. Our torches give a bit of light, but otherwise it's dark and gloomy. And cold. We step inside. It smells like every other church or chapel I've been in; wood and dust and hymn books. I quite like it. It reminds me of St David's Day in the Juniors when we'd go to Penuel to sing in the morning, then get the afternoon off. That was good.

But it's different now, because there's nothing good about mortgage payment day.

Catrin walks down the aisle to the front of the church. 'There's a door here with a little sign on it. Hang on ...' She goes up to it. 'Vestry. What's one of those?'

We go over. The vestry isn't locked. It's tiny and a bit warmer than the church. There's a small kitchen area with a sink and a camping stove, a comfy-looking chair and another door. In the corner is a tall mirror and a rail with robes on it.

'Looks like a staffroom for vicars,' I say.

'It is,' Tam says. 'Kind of.'

Catrin opens the other door. 'Toilet. That's good. I'm fed up of going in the bushes.' She turns to Jinx. 'You know what? I think staying here's a great idea.'

He grins. 'I bagsy the chair then.'

'Shouldn't Catrin have it?' Tam asks.

She folds her arms, looking a lot like her mother when her father says something twp. 'Why? Because I'm the girl?'

'Well, yeah.'

'I'm not a delicate little flower. I've matched you boys all the way so far, haven't I? I can handle the floor.'

'Women's Lib,' Jinx whispers to Tam. 'Just nod.'

'We'll do *Ip dip dip* for the chair,' I say.

We do it. I win.

We put our rucksacks down and make a little indoor camp, then search through our things to see what's left to eat.

'I'll put the kettle on for the Cup-a-Soups,' Tam says. 'Do you think it's stealing if we use a bit of the gas?'

'We could leave some money,' I say.

Tam nods and gets on with it.

'It's nobbling in here, 'I say. 'Time to get into my – oh heck.'

'What?' Catrin asks.

'I haven't got a sleeping bag.'

It's still in the Nant Copperworks. We all forgot. Not surprising really.

'Flaming Gary and Dean,' Jinx mutters.

'Gits,' Catrin says, her eyes narrowing. 'I hope they got lost in that tunnel. I hope there was a secret labyrinth in it and no one finds their withered bodies for years.'

Jinx watches her, unsure whether to laugh or be horrified.

She shrugs. 'Just saying.'

Tam pulls his sleeping bag out of his rucksack and offers it to me. 'Have mine.'

'But then *you'll* be cold,' I say.

'I could unzip mine,' Jinx says. 'If me and Tam cwtch up we can use it like a spread-out blanket. Sharing body heat helps – the SAS do it in extreme conditions.'

'You're having it.' Tam shoves his bag at me. 'No arguments. I owe you.'

I think he's still trying to make up for what he said about Richie, so I take it.

He turns to Jinx. 'We'll do what you say – except for the cwtching-up part. Obviously.'

We sit and dunk the last of the bread rolls into our mugs. They're stale now and the soup's watery, but it's good to have something warm. I'm starting to wonder if it's colder inside this church than out.

'Hey,' Jinx lifts his mug. 'Keep the village alive!'

Me and Tam clink our mugs with his and say it too. I go to take a sip, but Jinx shakes his head. 'No!' he says, his hand still raised. 'Wait for Catrin to say it.'

Her cheeks go a bit pink and she clinks her mug with ours. 'Keep the village alive.'

I'm smiling so much, it's hard to drink my soup.

Jinx says he's got an idea. Two – in fact – and goes out of the door. A minute later he's back, grinning over the top of a pile of those cushions people kneel on to pray. 'Nice these are … quite soft, if you squish them a bit … will do for pillows. Catrin, you can have the one with the dove on.'

'Tidy!' I say, catching the one he throws to me.

'I got some candles too, to save our torch batteries – ooh!'

He stops dead.

'What's up?'

'I don't know.' He takes one step back and then moves forward again, to the place he just was. 'It's much colder *here* –' he bends his knees to emphasise where he is – 'than *here*.' He steps back again. 'That's a sign of spirits, isn't it? Cold spots.'

'Shut up, Jinx,' Tam says.

'Probably just a draught or a vent or something,' I say. 'Sit down, mun.'

We perch on the cushions, in a little circle around a candle.

'It's like a séance,' Catrin says.

'We're not having one,' Tam mutters.

Jinx sighs. 'Be a good place though, wouldn't it?' He cocks his head towards the graveyard. 'Ghosts wouldn't have far to come.'

Catrin laughs.

'Know any spooky stories?' Jinx asks her.

'No, but I was thinking about that thing,' she says, pointing at the tall mirror. 'You know, the thing where you look in a mirror in the dark and say the devil's name three times and he appears behind you.'

Jinx goes to get up. 'I wonder if it works in a church.'

'Don't try!' I say. 'That freaks me out, that does.'

'Let's just get some kip,' Tam says, going over to the mirror and turning it to face the wall. 'And stop talking rubbish.'

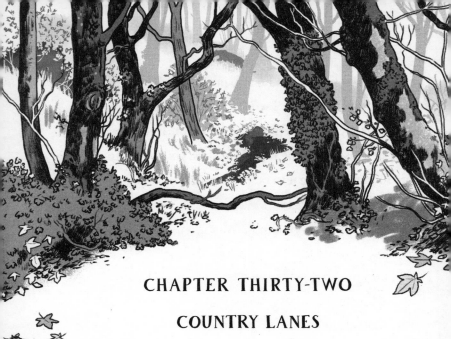

CHAPTER THIRTY-TWO

COUNTRY LANES

Even with cushions and a toilet, it hasn't been a restful night. It's Catrin and Jinx's fault, on about the devil and séances. Every time I heard a noise, I thought something evil was coming to get us.

Jinx flicks his torch on and throws back the sleeping bag. 'Bagsy me first wee!'

'Oi, mun!' Tam grunts and pulls it back over him.

'I was too scared to go in the night.' Jinx

sniggers. 'Busting, I am.'

Me and Tam sit up and I light a candle.

A snuffling noise comes from Catrin's sleeping bag. All I can see of her is the bobble from her hat sticking out of the top.

'You awake, Catrin?' I ask.

'Yeah,' she says grumpily. 'But I'm not moving until there's a cup of tea.'

Fair enough.

'What time is it?' Tam asks.

I look at my watch. 'Ten to six.'

Catrin grumbles and I'm pretty sure one of her words is rude.

'We can't hang about, can we?' I say. 'Someone could find us. Tea, then out.'

We make a big effort to leave the vestry as we found it, putting 10p in a collection box (for the gas and candles), and set off. Seeing the sun rising over our valley is amazing. The sky goes from black to navy and orange, finishing with icy blue. By the time we've

left the houses far behind and it really feels like countryside, it's light enough to switch our torches off.

'We need to look out for a phone box and then a
lightning tree,' Catrin says. 'When we see a lay-by on
the left, that's the field.'

The road is one of those narrow country lanes with
no pavements and only room for one car. Or tractor.
We squeeze into a spiky hedge to get out of the driver's
way. Right next to us, she stops and shouts over the
chug of the engine.

'Looking for that big cat, are you?'

We nod and she switches the engine off. 'Because
I know exactly where you'll find it.'

'*Do you?*' I ask, all excited.

'Yeah,' she says, leaning out of the cab towards us.
'But I can't shout it like, or everyone will know.'

We step up to the tractor. She jerks her head for us
to go even closer.

'Where is it?' Jinx whispers.

'See that field over there, the one with the sheep
in?' she says in a hushed voice. Our eyes all follow to

where her finger's pointing. 'Well, you go over the stile at the end, across two more fields and you'll get to a big tree. Oak it is. Go round that and you'll see a bank. Can't miss it, got loads of badger setts in it.'

'And it's there?' Catrin asks.

The woman sits back and nods, speaking louder now. 'Yeah. That's where the Beast of Blaengarw lives – right between the fairy house and the unicorn stable!' She roars with laughter and starts the engine again. 'Big cat – don't be so twp, mun!'

She drives off, clearly finding herself hilarious.

'Very funny!' Jinx says, whacking the hedge with his stick, then chucking it down the road after the tractor.

When we get to the lay-by, there's a red Mini parked in front of the gate. Two men are packing camping gear and professional-looking bags and camera cases into the boot. One of them's really tall with curly hair and the other one's small with a moustache. Mousy-looking, like a sidekick.

'Damn it,' Jinx mutters under his breath. 'What if we're too late?'

The men look up.

'Hello!' the curly one says, all friendly like. 'Looking for the Beast, are you?'

'Hope you have more luck than we did,' says his mate.

'Been here all night, we have.' Curly closes the boot. 'Nothing.'

Jinx turns to me. 'Maybe it's the wrong place after all?'

'Definitely not the wrong place,' the shorter man says. 'Look, we'll show you.'

'I'll catch you up, Paul,' says Curly.

The one called Paul flips the latch on top of the gate and lets us go through first. When we're all on the other side he waves his arm for us to follow him across the field. We reach a muddy patch and he points down.

'Paw prints!' Catrin says.

'Tracks of a big mammal,' Paul says. 'See by the depth of imprint? Had to be a decent weight.'

Jinx twties down. 'No sign of claw marks either. Can't be a dog, they can't retract their claws.'

Fair play, mind, he really does do his research.

'The Beast of Blaengarw,' the curly man says, joining us.

Tam frowns. 'If you're so sure it's the Beast, why are you leaving?'

Curly shrugs. 'Work.'

'Before you go,' I say. 'Have you seen two other kids? Boys. Our age.'

Paul shakes his head. 'Seen others, but not kids.'

They walk back to their car, waving and wishing us luck.

We've beaten Gary and Dean then. That's something.

CHAPTER THIRTY-THREE

COMPANY

We settle into a space under a big tree on the other side of the field; this way we can see if anyone else comes through the gate. Jinx gets out his binoculars and Catrin puts film in the camera. Now we wait.

And wait.

And wait.

'Hey, what's that over there?' Jinx points to a pale-coloured lump further down the field.

'Well, it's not a big cat,' Tam mutters.

Jinx gets up. 'No, but it could be a chicken carcass.'
He jogs off. When he reaches the lump, he nudges it
with his boot, then hurries back.

'False alarm.' He sits again.

'What was it?' Catrin asks.

He looks a bit sheepish. 'A Mother's Pride bread
bag.'

'Maybe the Beast likes a sandwich?' Catrin says.

Jinx grins. 'With chicken-flavour crisps in.'

She laughs. 'Of course.'

It's cold sitting under the tree. Hours pass and all me,
Tam and Catrin have really done is rub our arms and
wriggle our feet, trying to get warmer. But Jinx keeps
moving the binoculars, scanning the field and hedges
in the distance. He even makes us take a turn when
he eats his dinner.

'I thought searching for a big cat would be exciting,'
Tam says. 'But it's actually quite boring.'

'What did you expect?' Jinx puts the binoculars down. 'To be chasing it around? It's not a fox hunt. We don't want to scare or hurt it.'

'Yeah,' I say. 'We don't want it to know we're here.'

'What do you think will happen?' Catrin asks. 'When – if – we get a photo and have proof … you don't think anyone *will* hurt it, do you?'

'They might offer a new reward,' Tam says. 'For shooting it.'

'Tam!' she squeals, horrified.

'Nah, they'll put it in a zoo, I expect,' Jinx says.

'I don't like that idea much either. It living in a cage.'

'Well, whatever hap—' He groans. 'Oh God, we've got company.'

Gary and Dean are launching themselves over the gate.

'What do we do?' Catrin whispers.

'Stop them,' I say, getting up. 'We were here first. They can get lost.'

'Yeah,' Jinx says. 'I'm not having this!'

Catrin gets up too and we march towards Gary and Dean, who look annoyed, but not shocked, to see us.

'Well,' Gary sneers. 'Look who it is.'

'Go home,' I say.

'Oh no, North, that's not how this works. You need to disappear so we can get a photo, then we won't rip your heads off after all.'

I frown and rub my chin. 'Hmm, I thought you were going to smash them in, not rip them off.'

'Think you're so clever, don't you?' Dean says. He drops his bag and folds his arms. Gary does the same.

'Cleverer than you,' I say. 'But that's not saying much.'

Dean picks up a thick branch. 'You owe us for blocking that tunnel.'

I eye the branch. *He's not going to use it, is he?*

Then Tam's next to me. I glance sideways at him and he nods slowly, just once, and it feels good to have him with us. Properly with us.

We all fold our arms too. It's like a stand-off in a film.

'It's not here,' Tam says. 'The Beast.'

Gary smirks. 'That's not what we heard.' He jerks his thumb over his shoulder. 'Two blokes just stopped their Mini and told us this is the place.'

Paul and Curly. Damn it.

'Well, it's not,' Jinx says stupidly.

'Then why are *you* here? And why's she got a camera round her neck?'

They've got us there.

'Tell you what,' Dean says. 'Give us a go with it, and we'll call it quits.'

'No way,' I say. 'You need to leave. We were here first and there's four of us and two of you.'

'And I know judo,' Jinx says. *Oh God, why's he saying that? He only went three times when he was ten.*

Gary laughs and looks at Dean, almost like he's giving him a signal.

Then everything happens really fast.

CHAPTER THIRTY-FOUR

SCRAPPING

Dean lifts the branch and swings it high. High enough to go over our heads, but not Tam's. The whack is sickening. He lands with a thump. He's used to getting clattered on the rugby pitch and, for a stupid split second, I think he'll get straight up, but he only manages to reach all fours. His eyes are glazed. He doesn't have a clue what just happened or where he is.

Gary reaches out and yanks the camera strap, pulling Catrin towards the ground. I try to stop him, but Dean bats me away with one arm.

Before I can get my balance back, he's got Jinx in a strangle-hold.

Catrin tugs at Gary's arms, but she's on her knees now, her teeth gritted as she tries to fight him off. She's got no chance. Neither has Jinx. I look frantically from one to the other.

'Not me ...' Jinx gasps. 'Help Catrin!'

I leap behind Gary and grab his shoulders, twisting him, trying to make him let go. There's a thud and Catrin cries out.

The camera's snapped off its strap.

Dean lets go of Jinx, lunges forward and grabs the camera, ripping the back clean off and pulling out the film. It falls to the ground in shiny ribbons.

'Try and get a photo *now*,' he spits, flinging the broken casing into the bushes.

I look at Catrin and Jinx. Tears run down her face. He coughs and rubs his neck.

'You … filthy, stinking …' I can't find the words. 'I'll—'

'You'll *what*, North?' Gary laughs. 'Tell your *mammy and daddy*? Oh no – wait!' He looks right at me. 'You can't, can you?'

It's like someone flicked a switch and the blood in my veins has turned to ice water. Even Dean looks shocked.

I don't think any of us saw Tam getting up. He's wearing a look I've never seen on anyone's face before – it's pure calm and pure rage. He's completely in control. He knows he's already won. It's scary.

He lands a punch on Gary; a perfect upper cut which knocks him clean off his feet. It's like he's flying.

Tam turns slowly to face Dean, who bounces on his toes, hands in the air. 'All right, butty. No need for this, eh? Just let me past and we'll go.'

Tam steps to one side and Dean races off, grabbing Gary by the scruff and dragging him over the gate and away.

We all just stand here. Stunned.

213

Catrin watches me.

I can't breathe. All this. Tam knocked sideways, Jinx half strangled, Catrin's dad's camera. Tam's punch. And what Gary said.

What he said.

What he said.

My throat hurts. I can't swallow the lump away. My head feels light. Tears prick at my eyes.

I run and I don't look back.

My friends' voices reach me as if I'm underwater, the whooshing sound of my heartbeat in my ears making them distant and muffled. But I can just make out Catrin saying, 'Leave him.'

I run all the way down the field till I get to a fence, scramble to the top and fall to the ground on the other side. I keep going, across the track and on to a smaller lane.

The cold air rushes into my lungs but I feel hot under my parka. I have to run and run and run till all the misery and hopelessness have gone.

Maybe I'll need to run forever.

CHAPTER THIRTY-FIVE

THE SAME MOMENT

I don't run forever.

I stop at a dip in the hedge and stare down the valley. The river winds away back through Blaengarw and Craigwern and Ystradmawr all the way to Ponty.

All this way, all the things that have happened, and now, if the Beast of Blaengarw jumped on to Catrin's lap and purred it'd make no difference, because we're back to square one – no camera, no quest.

Why am I so stupid? Thinking a photo – some money – will make a difference. Even if we could pay the mortgage, Richie's still broken the law. Snook and his gang aren't going to let him off the hook just because he wants out. That was true before we even started this. What the hell were we thinking? We're just some kids who had a crazy idea we didn't think through. But we had to do something because doing nothing was too hard.

So, what's left?

Something moves by the hedge along the left side of the field. Big, fluid and dark against the green.

I blink and lean forward as far as I can, because … it can't be – can it?

But it is. A big cat. The Beast of Blaengarw.

It walks so slowly, the bones in its shoulders moving slinkily up and down. It's thicker-bodied than I thought it'd be, heavier and more solid. And it's coming towards me.

It sniffs and looks up with its mouth open in that funny vampire-way that pet cats do.

Then it sees me and we stare and stare and stare. But I'm not afraid. And I don't think the Beast is either. It's like it knows I won't bother it. We're just caught in the same moment. An agreement that we'll let each other go about our business. A kind of 'All right?' and carry on.

A thought hits me. A sudden, surprising thought. Even if I had the camera I wouldn't use it. Because the cat needs to be left alone. If it's been free and hiding for this long, I reckon it can stay that way. It knows how to survive in the world. Which is something me and Richie are going to have to learn to do.

It turns and stalks off.

Above us, the sky's turning purple and red. It'll be dark soon. I'd better get back to the others.

217

CHAPTER THIRTY-SIX

LANDY

When I reach the track, Catrin, Tam and Jinx are sitting on the gate, our bags in the lay-by at their feet. They jump off when they see me.

'All right, butt?' Jinx calls.

'Yeah.' I look at Tam. 'How's your head?'

'Sore.' He rubs it. 'But I'll live.'

'Calmed down, have you?'

He shrugs. 'Suppose. Think I must've been

holding that in for a while.'

'Well, it's out now.'

'You can say that again!' Jinx says, kind of in awe.

I turn to him and Catrin. 'What about you two?'

'We're all right,' she says. 'Aren't we?'

He nods.

We sling on our rucksacks and just stand here, all facing each other. It's Jinx who breaks the silence.

'We'll come back,' he says. 'Try again. We'll get another camera – I'll pinch Karen's if I have to – I know it's not fancy or anything, but it's better than nothing.'

Me and Tam stare at him like he's gone mad. Catrin scuffs the ground with the toe of her boot.

'What?' Jinx pleads. 'Come on. Tam? Catrin? We can't give up, can we? This is for Jason and Richie.'

'It's over, Jinx,' I say quietly.

Catrin glances at me and speaks softly to Jinx. 'We did our best, we really did, but—'

'No!' He's so loud it makes her jump. 'What's the

matter with you? You're meant to be his oldest friend, so he keeps flaming telling us!'

'That's not fair,' Tam says.

Jinx turns on him, his face all red under his bobble hat. 'And you! Give Gary Hall a smack and then what? Back to normal, is it? Whatever happened to "Leave no one behind"? *Nemo resideo*? Well, stuff the pair of you! *I'm* not letting Jason down. I'll come back on my own if I have to.'

He turns, but I grab his arm and force him to face me. 'It'll be okay.'

He kind of deflates like a punctured tyre. 'It won't though, will it? Not if you move away. You don't want to lose Richie, but we don't want to lose you. *I* don't want to lose you. You're my best friend. That's what all this is about, isn't it? Looking after your mates.'

'Aww, Jinx, mun.' Part of me wants to give him a cwtch like I do with Richie, but that'd be weird so I just grab his other arm and hold him here. 'You'll never lose me. No matter where I live.'

He nods sadly.

'Yeah.' Catrin sounds fake-cheery. 'But anything can happen yet. The miners might beat the government – or you might think of a new plan.' She smiles at him. 'You've got the brains for it.'

He manages a small smile back.

It's a miserable walk but we decide to go as far as we can before we drop with tiredness. No point staying up here now, and no point taking the river path. We'll stick to Top Road. I pass round the Polos and none of us says much.

When we get to the other side of Blaengarw we stop and look back at the sign.

I blow out a long breath. 'We tried, didn't we?'

'Yeah,' Tam says. 'And it's been fun in a way. Seeing Jinx running from that bull was brilliant.'

Jinx punches him on the arm. Tam rubs his sleeve. 'Oh, did a gnat just land on me? Where is it?' He pretends to look around for a tiny fly.

Jinx shakes his head. 'You ought to go on the

telly – *The Comedians* might have you, if they're desperate, like.'

The pavement is narrow and the road really winds in some places so we walk one behind the other. It might be quicker in miles, but it seems a lot longer. Coming up here felt kind of positive. We had a plan and quite a lot of stupidity but at least we had *something*.

What are me and my brother going to do now?

There's a low, growly engine rumble from behind us and a muddy old Land Rover passes. Then it slows and stops, hazard lights flashing in the dark. We stop too.

The driver – a man by the looks of it, and not a small one either – gets out, slams his door and crosses the road towards us.

Jinx grabs my arm. 'What if he's an axe murderer?'

'Shut up, you wally,' I say, but my stomach is squirming.

'I can't see an axe,' Tam says.

'Maybe it's in the back of the Landy,' Jinx says.

I grit my teeth. 'Shut *up*, mun!'

I shine my torch right on the driver. If he is an axe murderer it might put him off.

He waves a hand in front of his face. 'Hey, not trying to blind me, are you?'

'It's Maldwyn!' Catrin says.

'What the flaming hell are you lot doing now?' he calls.

'Going home,' Tam says.

Maldwyn looks at our pathetic faces. 'Ponty, isn't it? Come on then, I'll give you a lift.'

Land Rovers are not a smooth ride. Me, Tam and Jinx bump around in the back with our rucksacks while Catrin sits in the front and, avoiding any mention of Richie, tells Maldwyn how we got in this mess; how hard we tried, how Gary and Dean wrecked the camera, how all we can do now is go home.

'We failed,' she says sadly.

'You had a go though,' Maldwyn says in that too-jolly way adults do when they're trying to make you feel better about a failure.

She looks down in her lap.

'Important, wasn't it?' he says, less jolly now. 'This quest.'

Tam sighs. 'Yeah.'

Maldwyn catches my eye in the rear-view mirror. 'About more than money for sweets.'

I quickly look away.

CHAPTER THIRTY-SEVEN

THE WORKSHOP

The Landy echoes down Cae Terrace as Maldwyn pulls away. We watch it go.

'What now?' Tam asks.

'We find another way to help,' Jinx says.

I raise my eyebrows. 'Simple as that?'

'Well … yeah.' He looks at Catrin and Tam, who nod. 'That's what mates do.'

I turn to put my key in the front door. 'Just go home,

yeah?' I say quietly, feeling sick at the thought that, before long, this might not be my front door any more. Even the best friends in the world – and I have them, I already know that – can't help me and Richie now.

I don't even stop to listen to what they're saying. I need to see my brother, to confess where we've been and what we tried to do. Maybe it'll make him understand how much I need him to stop what he's doing. Then we can work out a way to fix things. Me and him together.

But the house is totally dark and totally cold.

'Richie?' I call out, throwing my rucksack on the floor. I grab my torch and run to each room. I look upstairs. But, of course, he's not here. He'll be with Snook Hall. Getting himself deeper in trouble.

I can't stand it. I need to see him. I don't care what happens to me now.

I yank the front door open, rush out without looking and bump straight into a human tree trunk. Tam, Catrin and Jinx look at me, worry all over their faces.

226

'Where you going?' Jinx asks.

'To find Richie.'

Before I can do anything to stop them, they throw their rucksacks into the passage on top of mine.

'*Nemo resideo*,' Tam says. 'Wherever you're going, we're going too.'

We stand together, peering down a gravel track leading off the Esgyn Road.

'My dad made you think the workshop is down *there*?' Catrin says.

I take a big breath. 'Yep.'

'Jase,' Tam says. 'Don't have a go at me or anything but … what are we going to do if Snook's there?'

'No idea.' I start down the track.

'Okay then.'

They walk with me.

The track runs through fields for about half a mile until it curves round to a high, metal gate. It's open, its chains and padlock hanging loose. I go to slip inside and feel a hand grab my shoulder.

Tam smiles in that annoying, calm way he does. 'We need to see what's going on first. Up there.' On the left, the land slopes to a high, grassy bank.

We sneak up and lie on our stomachs, commando-style, looking down at a big corrugated-iron building. Next to it a generator hums and rattles. Richie and Snook walk out on to a scruffy, concrete yard lit by the light from the workshop. Cars – and parts of cars – are dumped all over the place.

'Get on with that Cortina,' Snook says, screwing his face up as he takes a drag of his cigarette.

'It'll get done,' Richie says. 'It's taking longer because the equipment's rubbish.'

'A *bad workman blames his tools*. Ever heard that one, Richie-boy?' Snook laughs, going back to his own car. 'Just do it. Customer wants it tomorrow.'

'All right,' Richie says. 'But that blowtorch needs—'

Snook turns whip-fast and makes it across the yard in three big strides. He puts his arm across Richie's chest, grabbing him by the shoulder and slamming him against the corrugated-iron wall.

Catrin gasps.

'*Don't* tell me what we need, all right?' Snook pulls Richie towards him then slams him against the wall again. 'Shut your whining.'

I try to get to my feet but Tam grabs me and pins me down.

'Cortina!' Snook walks off, flicking his cigarette butt over his shoulder. 'Sort it. Today.'

Tam's actually sitting on me, his hand over my mouth. Stopping me from running down the slope, from ripping Snook Hall's stinking head off.

'He'll batter you,' Tam whispers in my ear. 'And then he'll batter Richie. Cool it.'

Snook gets in the car, revs the engine like he's such a big man and screeches off down the lane.

As soon as Tam gets off me, I spring up and fly down the slope, arms flailing like a crazy windmill.

Richie looks up. 'Jason? Jason! What the *hell*?'

CHAPTER THIRTY-EIGHT

TOGETHER

It's such a steep slope I can't stop when I get to the bottom. I run across the concrete and, just before I crash into the side of the workshop, Richie throws out an arm to catch me. I swing round and we end up in a sort of cuddle.

Then he holds me by the shoulders, at arm's length, and swears. A really bad one.

Next thing, my mates are with us, all panting

and looking edgy.

Richie glances down the lane. 'You can't be here.'

'No, listen …' I say.

'If he comes back …'

I'm scared by how nervous he looks.

'You don't know what you're risking by being here.' He looks around at us. 'All of you. Just go home.'

'*Richie!*' I'm practically shouting now. 'You have to get out of here too. You can come with us. Then we'll call the police – anonymously, like – and Snook and his gang will get arrested and no one has to know you were involved.'

'Jase.' He almost laughs. 'I'm in this up to my neck!'

'Tell them the truth then, that Snook forced you. They'll have to believe you. You've never been in trouble before.'

'It'll be okay, Richie.' Jinx turns to Tam and Catrin. 'Won't it?'

They nod, looking very serious.

'*Jesus Christ!*' Richie mutters. 'You stupid, *stupid* kids.'

I fold my arms. 'We're not going without you.'

'This isn't a game, Jason, mun, this is real life!'

'Then why are you messing it up? You're meant to be the grown-up!' The last part comes out scratchy and strangled, because I'm trying not to cry.

Tam, Jinx and Catrin move away from us.

'Listen,' Richie says, his voice much softer now. 'I don't feel any more grown up than you do.' He runs his hands through his hair. It stays up in scruffy little spikes. He looks down the track again. 'You can't be here.'

'What's that smell?' Jinx asks, looking around. 'It's a bit smoky.'

'Snook just had a fag.' Richie turns away from me. 'Go home.'

'It's not cigarettes,' Catrin says. 'It's sort of chemical.'

'There's loads of stuff like that round here.' He looks behind him, at a pile of oily rags. 'Just – oh Christ!'

The rags are smouldering.

232

Before any of us can even think, they go up with a whoosh of flames. We jump back, all except Richie, who runs to the back of the workshop.

What's he doing?

The flames catch a newspaper hanging over the edge of a workbench, spread to a calendar on the wall. It's all so fast.

'Richie!' I look at the spray cans and oil and – oh God – is that a welder's gas tank? *'Get out of there!'*

He's rummaging on a shelf. 'I'll be there now!'

'No!'

A wave of heat flows towards me and hands pull me backwards. Further away from my brother.

'Someone go and ring the fire brigade!' I shout.

'But …' Jinx splutters. 'The police will know Richie's—'

'For God's sake! I'd rather have him in jail than dead! Run!'

But Tam's already gone.

'Where is it?' Richie's voice is full of panic. 'Where the hell – oh! Got it!'

'*Richie!*' My yell is more like a scream.

He faces us now. But in that half a minute it took for him to find whatever it was, the flames are too high for him to pass.

'Where's the fire extinguisher?' Jinx screeches, looking around desperately.

Richie's a mixture of fear and rage. 'There isn't one! Just get away! Move back!'

Catrin holds on to my arm. Me, her and Jinx stare at the flames and, through them, at Richie backed up against the wall. 'Tam'll be at the phone box in no time,' she whispers. 'No one could get there faster than him.'

'It's all right!' I shout to Richie. 'Tam's gone for help!'

A gust of wind whips around the workshop, swirling smoke and tiny bits of ash towards us. We jump back, coughing.

'There's so much in there that's flammable,' Jinx splutters.

I turn on him. 'Shut up! Shut your mouth! He's going to be okay!'

He blinks. 'I'm sorry, Jase. I only meant … I … I …'

Richie's pulling things off the shelving at the back – paint pots and spray cans and cloths. He throws them to the far corner, away from the fire, and goes to the side of the shelving and heaves at it till it falls. He leaps out of the way.

Then I see it, through the flames and the smoke. A doorway! There's a back door!

'He'll be all right,' Catrin says. 'He can get out!'

Richie pulls at the handle but nothing happens. He puts one foot against the corrugated-iron wall and jerks and tugs, but the door's not budging.

He turns back to us, and the look on his face terrifies me. My heart feels like it's going to explode. My brother is stuck in a burning building with chemicals and gas tanks and petrol.

'Don't give up!' Jinx shouts. 'Keep pulling!'

Then it comes to me – I run. Around the side of the workshop to the back. The door is rusted shut. The ground around the base of it thick with grass and weeds and piled-up dirt. I hack at it with the heel of my boot, scraping it away.

'Richie?' I shout.

Richie coughs. 'Jason?'

'You pull, I'll kick! Ready?'

'Ready!'

I kick and kick and kick. All my best Bruce Lee moves, all the strength I've got. I kick and kick and kick.

I can't do it, can hardly dent it. I'm not strong enough.

But then the door buckles as it jerks free on one side. Richie's fingers reach around it and he pulls.

Catrin and Jinx join me, and then Tam's here. We all put our shoulders to the door and push.

'Hurry up!' Richie shouts. He coughs and coughs.

I push even harder. I don't know how I do it, but I do.

'The metal's getting warmer!' Catrin cries.

Oh God.

We shove like crazy, our feet slipping and skidding on the ground.

'This isn't working,' Tam says, stepping back. 'Richie! Get out of the way!'

'What are you doing?' I yell.

'All of us … together,' he pants. 'One move … like a battering ram. On three.'

Me, Jinx and Catrin step back too.

Tam counts. 'One … two … three.'

Smash!

The door caves inwards and Richie stumbles out in a haze of smoke. We run to the top of the grassy bank and lie down, panting and heaving and coughing.

'The fire engine's on the way,' Tam says, through gasps. He looks at my brother. 'You could run away. We'd never tell.'

But Richie shakes his head. 'It's over.'

He grabs me and pulls me into a massive cwtch, kissing the top of my head for ages, then resting his cheek on me. 'And it's going to be okay. One way or another.'

I nod, which is difficult when you're squashed in a bear hug, and hold him tight. I sob. Properly sob; screwed-up face, stupid noises. The whole lot. And I don't even care that Tam and Jinx are here.

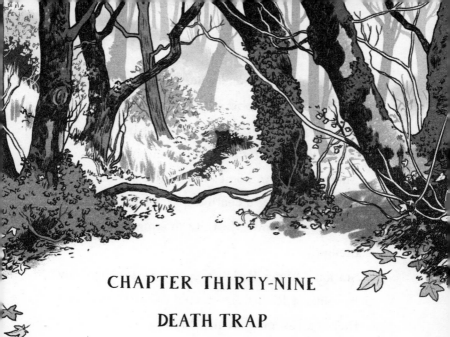

CHAPTER THIRTY-NINE

DEATH TRAP

We see the flashing lights and hear the siren from miles away. Richie tells us to stay up on the bank while he goes to meet them but, of course, none of us listen.

The firemen put the fire out really fast. Now one of them – the one who was giving orders to the others – comes over.

'Right then. I'm Station Officer Parisse.' He takes

his helmet off and tucks it under his arm. 'Time to tell me what happened and why five kids are up here in the middle of it.'

Five? Oh, he means Richie.

Another fireman comes out of the smoking workshop. 'That place is a death trap. It's amazing it hasn't gone up before now. Most of the equipment in there is ancient.'

Station Officer Parisse's eyebrows scrunch down as he looks at Richie. 'Do I need to call the police?'

Richie takes a big breath. 'Yeah.'

'It's not his fault!' I say. 'They made him. And we needed the money – he'd never have done it otherwise.'

'Shush, Jase,' Richie mutters, putting his arm round my shoulders and giving me a weak smile. 'I can handle this.'

Parisse looks from me to Richie. 'Brothers, are you?'

'Yeah,' we say together.

'Well, Jase … Jason is it?' he asks. I nod. 'Leave it

240

to me and your big brother, eh? Oi, Tom!' he calls over his shoulder. 'Take these four out of the way, will you?'

I fold my arms.

Richie lets go of me. 'Go on. I'll be okay.'

Grudgingly I go with the fireman called Tom and my mates to the other side of the yard. A car comes down the track and part of me hopes it's Snook coming back – so he can get caught right here in front of us – but I know he's not that stupid. Instead, a brown Ford Escort pulls up on the concrete.

I know that car.

'It's my dad!' Catrin says.

Nigel just hangs over the steering wheel for a minute, staring up at the smouldering workshop. Then he looks around at all the people and fixes on us. His car door flies open. 'Catrin!'

'You know these children?' Tom asks.

'This is my daughter,' Nigel says. 'What in God's name have you lot been up to now?'

'I can explain,' she says.

'You're going to have to – I saw the flames from Park Street!'

'Sorry.'

'You didn't start this, did you?' Nigel looks at the fire engine. 'Please tell me you didn't start a fire.'

'We didn't, Dad. Honest!'

He nods towards Richie. 'I was really hoping I was wrong and he wouldn't be here.' He turns to Tom. 'I don't normally drive towards burning buildings.'

'The important thing is they're all right,' Tom says.

Catrin wraps her arms around her dad and bursts into tears. Nigel kind of melts. He looks over the top of her head to Richie and Parisse, then back to me. 'Your brother in trouble?'

I nod.

Nigel gives me that look. The concerned one. 'Are *you*?'

I shrug. 'Probably.'

'No,' says Tom. 'But he needs to go home. They all do. Couldn't take them, could you?'

'I'm not going anywhere without Richie.'

'You're coming home with us,' Nigel says.

I feel Tam's hand heavy on my shoulder. 'Come on, Jase. It really is all over now.'

'Give me a minute.'

I walk over to Richie and Parisse. They stop talking. 'Nigel says I have to go to their house. But I won't if you need me.'

'I don't want you to see me getting taken off in a police car.' Richie pulls me into a cwtch. 'Go home, little brother.'

'Love you,' I say.

'Love you too.'

CHAPTER FORTY

FREAKING OUT

Nigel drops the boys off first. Jinx's mother goes spare, can't believe her golden boy could get himself in so much trouble. Tam's father is calm and polite, not showing much, which I reckon is worse. Bethan and Nigel make me and Catrin go straight up to bed and say they'll deal with us in the morning.

Which is worst of all.

I know I won't get a wink, on the floor of Rhodri's

bedroom, with him snuffling like an asthmatic hamster and all the thoughts whizzing around in my brain.

But as soon as my head's on the pillow, my whole body feels that nice sort of heavy which drags you into sleep. Maybe it's exhaustion. Maybe it's relief. Because there is a bit of that – relief that Richie's doing the right thing now, he just made some bad choices. But losing both your parents can do that to you. Catrin has the scar to prove it.

It was the best sleep I've had in ages.

At the breakfast table, Rhodri's got his head over his cereal bowl, listening for the snap, crackle and pop.

'Eat them up,' Bethan says. 'Michael and his mother will be here soon, to take you to the park.'

'But I want to know why Jason had to sleep in my bedroom,' he says, wiping milk off his ear.

'Never you mind.'

I stir the Rice Krispies around my bowl, wondering

what breakfast is like in prison. They call it *doing porridge*. Maybe that's all they get.

It takes over an hour to tell Bethan and Nigel everything. I'm scared they'll kick me out, ban me and Catrin from being friends, but, while they're not exactly happy, they seem more *worried* than anything.

'Is that it?' Bethan asks. 'You're not keeping anything else from us?' We shake our heads. 'No stolen jewels under your bedroom floorboards? No gold bullion in the coal bunker?'

She's trying to show she's not angry, to make us feel better, but only Richie coming home could do that.

Nigel grabs his car keys and says he's heading down the police station. I stand up.

'No, boy,' he says. 'You stay here. I'll ring if there's any news.'

'But—'

'No buts, it's not a place for you. Anyway, you need to be here for your Aunty Pearl.'

'*Aunty Pearl? Why's she coming?*'

'I rang her,' Bethan says. I open my mouth to protest but she looks suddenly stern. '*No, Jason*. You have lost any right to complain about this. She's your family – as good as – and she needed to know.'

I slump on the table. Aunty Pearl. She'll go mad.

She turns up at half nine, with rollers in her hair and a headscarf over them. Aunty Pearl hates it when ladies go out of the house like that. She must have been in a very angry rush to jump on a bus in that state.

'Jason, bach!' she says. 'What on earth have you and your brother been getting yourselves into? The police! Fire engines! Sneaking off up the valley to goodness-knows-where!'

Catrin offers to take her coat but she waves her away and keeps on. 'I can't believe it, I really can't! I knew this would happen.' She shakes her head and her rollers wobble about. 'I said all along two boys like you can't cope on your own. And now look at the mess you're in!'

'Make your mind up,' I mutter under my breath.

'*Pardon?*'

My face feels hot and my heart pounds and I know I shouldn't say it, but part of me really doesn't care. It's not going to make a difference to how much trouble I'm in.

'I said make your mind up.' I lift my head and look right at her. 'You just said you can't believe it, then you said you knew it would happen. Which is it, because it can't be both.'

'*Jason,*' Bethan warns. 'That's enough.'

Aunty Pearl puts her hand over her heart like I wounded her. 'If your mother could hear you now.'

I jump up, banging my leg on the table. 'But she can't, can she? Neither can Dad! So you're still not making sense! Because if they were here, none of this would have happened!'

She gasps. 'Oh, bachgen,' she says quietly. 'Oh my poor, poor boy.'

What's going on?

Aunty Pearl clutches the buttons of her coat. 'It's my fault, Jason. I've let you down.'

I have no idea what to say.

Bethan and Catrin leave the kitchen, edging away quietly.

'I should have come over more,' Aunty Pearl says. 'Given your brother support instead of criticising all the time.'

'But why would you? Why would you suddenly give Richie a chance to be this grown-up you expect him to be? Well, we'll be fine – we've got Bethan and Nigel. They care. We don't need you.'

It's her turn to be speechless. She takes a deep breath, looking up at the ceiling. Then she sniffs. 'You think I don't care?'

I shrug.

'Oh Jason, I do care, but I went about it all the wrong way.' She sighs. 'I miss them too, you know … Your mother was my favourite godchild. I remember her being born – beautiful baby she was. Like an angel.'

I don't know what to do. She's never ever been like this with me – talking about feelings and things – it's making me feel weird.

Her voice is a whisper. 'I never thought I'd live to see her go before me.'

Standing here in her rollers and overcoat, she looks so old. And so sad. I haven't really stopped to think about how she might feel. She's grieving too, and trying to help us in her own, nagging Aunty Pearl-type way. And Mam always said she had a good heart, deep down. Suppose it's not buried as deep as I thought.

'You weren't that bad,' I mutter.

'Jason love, I threw your magazines in the bin!'

'Richie got them back,' I say. 'And only one was too smelly to keep.'

'Well,' she says, wiping her face with the back of her hand. 'I'm sorry. I can see now how much he does for you.'

I tap my pockets. 'Erm … do you need a hanky?'

I don't even have a hanky. I've never had a hanky. I don't know what I'm saying.

She shakes her head. 'What's important now is what we do next. If Bethan will let me, I'll ring the police station. See if there's any news about Richard.'

'Okay.'

She taps on the living-room door. I hear muffled voices, then, in the passage, the click of the receiver and sound of her dialling.

Catrin comes into the kitchen. 'You all right?'

'Yeah,' I say. 'Making a bit of a habit of freaking out, aren't I?'

'I think you're allowed to freak out, to be honest.' She crosses over to the biscuit barrel. 'Mam says we can have a Wagon Wheel each. Just don't tell Rhodri.'

CHAPTER FORTY-ONE

FISH FINGER SANDWICHES

It's been the longest few days of my life. And that's saying something. Me and Catrin sit on her front doorstep, not caring that it's cold. I can't stand being inside, just waiting for the phone call. Aunty Pearl's in our house doing what she does best – cleaning – but she's not being a pain about it.

Richie had to go to court, but the police got him in front of the magistrate quickly because he was helpful and didn't try to make out like he was innocent. He wouldn't let me see him in custody, so Nigel kept visiting.

Bethan brings us warm milk, and cushions to sit on. Rhodri wants me to play with him but I say not today. He doesn't even complain. I must look properly miserable.

'Want to get our bikes?' Catrin asks. 'Just up and down the street? Might take your mind off it.' I look at her like she's gone mad. 'Sorry, I know nothing really will.'

I stare into my mug. 'You get yours if you like.'

'I'll stay here,' she says quietly. 'Next to you.'

Next to me. By my side. Where she's always been.

Aunty Pearl leans out of our front bedroom window. 'When's the last time you washed these nets?'

'Oh my God, Catrin – she's taking the flipping curtains down!'

Catrin leans forward and looks up at our house. 'She's crackers, mun.'

'I don't know!' I shout to Aunty Pearl.

She says nothing and closes the window.

The phone rings. We jump, slopping our milk. I run into the passage to answer it.

'Richie?'

Pip pip pip while he puts the money in.

'Hello? Jason, is that you?'

'Yeah. What happened?'

'It's all right. I got bail. Nigel's been brilliant.'

I nod. Stupidly, like he can see me.

'Jase? You still there?'

'Y-yeah.' I can't seem to get any other words out.

'See you soon, yeah? After the paperwork. Love you.'

'Love you too.'

Click.

A weird, wobbly rush of air comes out of me and I sit down hard on the telephone chair.

'Well?' Bethan's in the kitchen doorway.

'He's coming home,' I whisper.

It's way after teatime when they come through the front door, not that I ate much. Too jumpy. Nigel smiles, but it's an exhausted one. Richie follows him in, shoulders slumped, looking completely worn out.

Bethan says she'll do us fish finger sandwiches. 'And a nice cup of tea,' she says, giving Richie a cwtch.

He manages a smile too. 'Thanks.'

'Catrin,' she says. 'Your brother's meant to be asleep but he's scampering around up there. Tell him to get in bed right now. Read him a story, that might settle him down.'

Catrin huffs but goes upstairs. Me and Richie get ushered into the living room.

'Where's Aunty Pearl?' he asks, looking around as if he expects her to pop up from behind a chair.

'Gone home to pay the coalman,' I say. 'What happened?'

'She been all right?'

'Yeah, fine, but never mind her – what happened, Rich?'

'Sit down and I'll tell you.' He flumps on to the

255

settee and rubs his hand over his forehead. 'Shattered, I am.'

I pull the pouffe across the room so I can sit facing him. 'Did they treat you okay? Are you going to proper prison?'

'Slow down, Jase! Give me a chance, mun. I'll tell you now.'

I sit up straight and fold my arms. 'Go on then.'

'It has to go to Crown Court –'

'Like on the TV?'

He smiles a bit. 'Yeah, but no cameras. The police think I have a very good chance of avoiding a prison sentence. Because I've shown remorse and because, well …' He picks some fluff off his best trousers. 'There are mitigating circumstances.'

'What does that mean?'

He takes a big breath. 'It means they can see it's out of character for me – Nigel, Gwyn and Dai Dep being character witnesses helped, especially Dai – and that I've been under pressure since Mam and Dad died.'

'Oh.'

He leans forward and takes both my hands in his. 'Not because of you though. Don't go thinking that.'

'I know.'

'And I thought money was the answer,' he says, looking down at our fingers. 'That if we had enough, then Aunty Pearl would see we were fine and get off my case and ... well ... I wanted to look after you ...' He sighs. So long and heavy and sad I feel my heart squish up in my chest. 'Like Mam and Dad would've wanted.'

I blink and tears roll down my cheeks.

'I have to testify against Snook and the gang.' He lets go of my hands and goes to get up. 'But I don't want to think about that right now. Let's talk about the rest tomorrow, eh? I'm starving.'

But I put my hand on his arm. 'What did you go back for?'

He looks confused.

'In the workshop, when the fire started. What did you go back for?'

He reaches inside his jumper. 'This.'

'Your St Christopher!'

'Took it off while I was working. Habit from the depot. Being safe. Which was a joke up there, I know.' He tucks it away again.

'That was a stupid thing to do. You could have died.'

'Been making a lot of stupid choices lately, haven't I?'

'Yeah.'

He looks me right in the eye. 'But it all stops here. I promise.'

And I believe him so all I say is, 'Let's go and eat. Those fish fingers smell lush.'

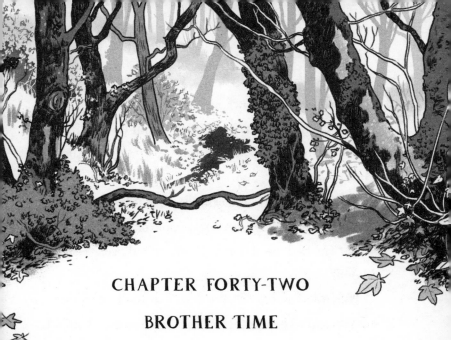

CHAPTER FORTY-TWO

BROTHER TIME

Richie opens the flask and pours us a cup of hot squash each. We sit on the mountain, on a fallen tree trunk, looking down over Ponty. From here we can see all the places we've known our whole lives. The river rushes round bends, smashing over rocks, making foamy splashes. It's high today because it rained a lot in the night. I wonder where Jinx's map is now; floating in the sea, I suppose.

'This is nice, isn't it?' Richie says. 'Just you and me.'

'Yeah.' I blow on my squash.

'We should do it more often. It can be our Bloke Time.'

'Brother Time.'

He nods once and smiles. 'All right. Brother Time. Jase?' He's got a funny look on his face, like when he had to tell me about the diesel. I don't like it.

'What?'

'We can't keep going on the way we are. I might have got out of that spot of bother ...'

I raise my eyebrows.

'Okay then, that *whole load* of bother, but it doesn't mean there's more money. And the bank definitely won't help us now I've got a criminal record.'

'Are we losing the house?'

He screws up his face and stares down the valley. 'Not if Aunty Pearl moves in. Permanently, like.'

'What? Live in Ponty?'

'She's prepared to sell her house and help us out.

That's a big thing, you know, especially at her age.' He eyes me sideways. 'What do you think?'

I watch the steam rise from my squash. Aunty Pearl. Before all this, I'd have said she was the worst option but, really, she might be the only way for us to stay together. And she's already a bit less naggy than she was.

'What if the three-day week ends soon and she sells her house for no reason?'

'I was struggling before that. My wages aren't like Dad's were, and the savings they left us soon went.'

'Why didn't you tell me?'

'Thought I could handle it … I know, I know … Look how that turned out.' He takes another drink. 'We can't keep the house on our own.'

Silence.

It's like a heavy weight hanging between us.

'Say something, Jase.'

I hold my cup tight, letting the warmth seep through my gloves into my hands, and think of what he said up at the workshop; about not feeling like a grown-up. He needs some time to be a teenager. Time to grieve, I suppose. If Aunty Pearl comes it won't be easy, but at least we can be proper brothers again.

I put my cup down. 'I think she should move in.'

He leans back to look at me, smiling slightly. 'Really?'

I smile back. 'Really.'

'I've done some pretty idiotic things, haven't I?' he says.

I shrug. 'You're not the only one.'

I tell him about the quest. He's not happy about some of it – the bull and the hay bales and Gary and Dean – but he laughs when I tell him about shutting them in the tunnel.

'Catrin and the boys did all that with you?' he asks.

I nod. 'For us, yeah.'

'Wow.' He blinks. 'Never stop being mates with them, Jase.'

'Believe me, I won't.'

CHAPTER FORTY-THREE

LAST ONE TO THE WASTE GROUND

There's a loud knock at the front door.

'I'll get it!' I race out of my bedroom.

'Don't run on the stairs!' Aunty Pearl calls from the kitchen.

'Sorryyyyyy!' I don't slow down though, just jump the last three with a sideways twist, landing neatly on the doormat. Not bad, if I say so myself.

I open the door to find Tam and Jinx, their bikes on

263

the pavement behind them.

'Coming out?' Jinx asks.

I turn and yell down the passage. 'Aunty Pearl, please can I go out on my bike?'

'Is your room tidy?' she asks.

'Yeah,' I shout back. I mouth *No* to the boys, shaking my head. They snigger.

'I suppose,' she calls. 'Be back for tea, mind.'

'I'll bring my bike round.'

When I go through the kitchen, Aunty Pearl's elbow-deep in the ironing basket. 'So, bach, if I go up to your bedroom, I'll find it spick and span, will I?' She gives me a pretend-stern look, the one where her eyes seem annoyed but her lips are smiling.

'Ermm ...' I say, my voice going up. 'Spicker and spanner than it was?'

'In other words, you picked your socks up for a change.'

'Just one sock.' I kiss her on the cheek and go out of the back door. 'But it's a start!'

I hear her laughing to herself as steam hisses from the iron.

By the time I get down our back lane and round to the front of the houses, Tam's riding up and down the road, doing brilliant skids. Jinx's bike is still on the pavement.

'Come on then,' I call. 'Waste ground, is it?'

'Hang on!' Jinx shouts. He doesn't get on his bike, just stands there like a lemon. What's he waiting for?

I ride down to him, getting there the same time as Tam, who pulls another skid, showering us with grit.

'Oi, mun!' Jinx says, but Tam only laughs.

Then I notice Catrin's front door is slightly open. I hear rushing footsteps and she appears, looking a bit pink and excited.

'My mother said yes, so I'll fetch my bike and meet you at the end of the road, yeah?' She grins at me and it's the biggest smile I've ever seen on her face. 'I'll be there now in a minute.'

She shuts the door.

'You called Catrin?' I don't know why I say it like a question, because it's pretty obvious he did.

Jinx nods.

'To come down the waste ground?'

'Yeah,' Tam says.

'She's one of us now, isn't she?' Jinx jumps on his bike and tears off yelling, 'Last one to the waste ground has to marry Mrs Fletcher!'

Catrin rides around the corner and we all pelt down the hill together.

The four of us.

WHERE THE '70S TAKES US ...

The 1970s might seem like a very long time ago, but – for me – it's not so historical. This story is set in February 1974, when I was four years old. I can't remember much about that actual month, but I do remember a lot about the decade and, with a bit of help from others, I was able to write this book.

So what was it like in Britain in 1974? For one thing, there was rationing. Yes! Just like with food and clothes during wartime – but in this year it involved energy. People couldn't turn on their lights or run a bath whenever they wanted. There were many reasons for this – long, complicated reasons – but the one most related to Jason's story is that miners went on strike for better pay and safer working conditions. This meant that there wasn't enough coal to produce electricity and heat buildings so, while the government and miners were trying to reach an agreement, many businesses ran for only three days per week.

Those hard times meant that Jason and Richie needed money. And each of them chose a different way to get it. For Jason the newspaper reward seemed like the answer. By today's standards, £100 (even though it's still a lot of money) might not seem enough to help pay for a house. But ... remember ... in the 1970s you could buy things for ½p. Yes, half a penny! Not a house, obviously, but more than one sweet!

All this was the backdrop for my story, but what I wanted to write about most of all was a group of friends who search for something and who, in the process, learn new things about themselves and each other. But ... what could they search for?

I've always been interested in people who claim to have seen strange creatures – like a large wild cat –

in unexpected places. Now we call these urban myths – tales which people insist are true, saying that it happened to someone they know. The Welsh valley setting fitted this well – I know from growing up in one that they're brilliant places for rumours to spread! The quest could begin …

I hope you enjoyed journeying back to the 1970s with Jason, Catrin, Jinx and Tam, and being part of their adventure.

lesley

ACKNOWLEDGEMENTS

I'd like to send my huge thanks to:

My incredible editor Zöe Griffiths and all at Bloomsbury Children's Books, especially Beatrice Cross, Jade Westwood-Studden, Isi Tucker and Fliss Stevens – I'm so proud to be part of your team.

Amber Caravéo, my superb agent – for endless support and fun chats.

Illustrator David Dean and Creative Director Stephanie Amster for yet another gorgeous cover.

All the booksellers, bloggers, reviewers, librarians, teachers, TAs, authors and illustrators who have supported me and my books.

Ged Potter for the invaluable information on police procedures, and to Tracy for the tea which kept us fuelled.

James at Derby London Camera Exchange for

helping me distinguish my K1000 from my Spotmatic SP500.

All the friends who have cheered me on in so many ways. Special thanks must go to Phil Earle and Emma Carroll for being so keen to read, and providing wonderful prepublication quotes.

My husband, Jon ... your reckless childhood deeds (and blatant disregard for your own safety) contributed so much to this story. You're lush and I love you.

My readers – knowing you're out there helps me do what I do.

PERSONAL ACKNOWLEDGEMENT

Someone I've already thanked deserves her very own page, and that's my editor, Zöe Griffiths.

You've been patient, insightful, kind and fun. My books are what they are because of you and I think you're brilliant.

And now you're off being brilliant elsewhere.

But no matter what happens in the future you will always be my first editor, and I believe that's a special thing. You've guided me through so much and I'll be forever grateful to have worked with you. That you share my love of rugby, strongman competitions, snooker and made-for-TV Christmas films was just the cherry on top of an already delicious cake!

For all the times you told me I've got this … Diolch, Zöe – it's been a blast!

273

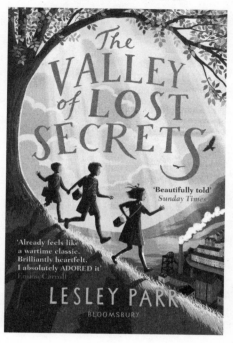

CHAPTER ONE

A DIFFERENT TYPE OF COUNTRYSIDE

There isn't as much sky as I thought there'd be. And what I can see is clear and blue, not the never-ending rain clouds we were told we'd get in Wales.

The guard blows his whistle and the train hoots back. I watch it pull away and my heart squeezes a bit. I want to get back on. I don't know why; it's not as if it's going back to London.

We've been through three stations today – from Paddington to Cardiff Central to here. This one's tiny, with only one platform. It's like our lives are shrinking. I straighten Ronnie's tag and we join the back of the line.

Dad said we'd be able to see for miles and miles in the countryside. He got us some library books with pictures of fields and hedgerows with little houses dotted around. But this isn't like that.

Massive, looming bulges of land – mountains, I suppose – have stolen most of the sky. I turn on the spot. They're all around, as though the village was dropped into the middle of a big fat cushion. Before now, the closest thing to a mountain I'd ever seen was a sand dune on Camber Sands. And it wasn't green. And it didn't have houses stuck on the side of it.

There's a tug at my sleeve. Ronnie's looking at me, eyes wide and teary. I lean down so he can whisper in my ear.

'This isn't like the pictures,' he says, sniffing.

'I know.'

'But Dad said—'

'He didn't know, did he? He didn't know we were coming here. He just knew it wasn't a city.' I look around again. 'There must be different types of countryside.'

'Well, this is the wrong type.' Ronnie sticks out his bottom lip.

This is all I need – a sulky little brother. No one will pick us if he looks a proper misery guts.

'Be quiet and try to look like a nice boy,' I say, making sure the string of his gas mask box sits properly on his shoulder. 'Nice and smart.'

I look over his head to the far end of the platform. The smoke's thinning, but it still stings my eyes and catches in my throat. I can see the face of the station clock now; it's almost teatime. The sign is clear too:

LLANBRYN

Funny word. Too many Ls.

Here we are, a wriggling, squiggling line of school-children. Duff's at the front with his little sister. She's even younger than Ronnie; too young to understand any of this. I can't see many faces; most are looking at our teacher, Miss Goodhew. Some of us seem excited, some curious, but I bet everyone's nervous. Even the ones pretending not to be. Maybe even Duff.

Ronnie's crying again. It's OK for little brothers to cry but big brothers have to be the brave ones. Not that I would cry, anyway. I'm twelve. He watches sadly as a guard puts our suitcases in a pile near the gate at the end of the platform.

'I want my Dinky van,' he splutters.

'You can't have it. It's packed. You know what Nan said.'

'But—'

'Ronnie, it's safe,' I say. 'Remember how well you wrapped it in your pyjamas? You did a really good job there.'

He nods and blinks back more tears. I know he's trying to be brave too.

Next to the guard, Miss Goodhew is talking to a man and a woman. The man is tall and has a thick overcoat buttoned over his large stomach, and he's got the biggest moustache I've ever seen. The woman's all done up like she's in her Sunday best. She's walking down the line now, giving out custard creams as she

4

counts us. When she gives one to Lillian Baker, Lillian thanks her for having us in their village. Duff's close enough to pull her plaits but he doesn't. He's not usually worried about getting into trouble; perhaps he *is* nervous. I bet Lillian Baker will get picked first. She's got long dark hair and her socks never fall down and all the grown-ups say she's pretty.

When the woman hands a biscuit to Ronnie, she stops and wipes away his tears with her hanky. She's got a metal badge pinned to her coat that says *WVS Housewives Service Identification*.

'What's your name?' she asks. Ronnie gulps and says nothing.

Now that she's close, I can smell lavender and peppermints. She lifts Ronnie's tag and says, 'Ronald, now that's one of my favourite names, that is.'

'We call him Ronnie,' I say, a bit harder than I mean to.

But she keeps on smiling, eyeing my tag. 'And you're a Travers too. Ronnie's brother, is it? So are you a James or a Jimmy?'

'Jimmy.'

'All right then,' she says. She gives me a custard cream and moves back up the line.

'She smells like Nan,' Ronnie whispers. His lip's wobbling again, so I take his hand and give it a squeeze, just like Dad would do.

'Eat your biscuit,' I say.

Miss Goodhew claps her hands and calls out to us. We all go quiet.

'These nice people are Mr and Mrs Bevan,' she shouts down the platform, using her fake-posh voice. 'They are here to take us up to the institute.'

I wonder what an institute is. It sounds grim.

'Welcome to Llanbryn!' Mr Bevan booms. I'm not surprised he booms. He looks like a boomer.

I glance at the sign again. It doesn't look like it says what *he* just said. Ronnie's copying him, screwing up his face, trying to make his mouth fit around the letters.

'Lll … clll … cllaaa …'

'Stop it,' I whisper. 'No one will pick us if they think you're simple.'

'Don't worry about your cases,' Mr Bevan says. 'We've got men taking them up for you.'

Ronnie tightens his grip on my hand and I know he's thinking about his Dinky van again. Those men – whoever they are – had better be careful with his case. If he loses that van, he won't stop crying till the end of the war.

We set off, our gas mask boxes bumping against us. Mrs Bevan and Miss Goodhew chat at the head of the line. Mr Bevan waits as we cross the road outside the station, then joins Ronnie and me at the back.

'Are you ready for your adventure, boys?' he asks, grinning.

What's he talking about? Adventures happen in jungles or on raging rivers or in the Wild West. Not here. Not in Wales with a whimpering little brother and a custard cream.

Ronnie's stopped crying, so that's something. He's twisted the top off his biscuit and is licking the creamy bit.

'Are we going up there?' he asks, his eyes darting nervously from Mr Bevan to the mountainside houses.

Mr Bevan nods. 'We are.'

'It's a long way up,' Ronnie says.

Mr Bevan turns to the houses and tilts his head from side to side. A big grin breaks out on his face, stretching his moustache and making him look like a happy walrus.

'Not for a big strong boy like you!'

Ronnie beams.

'Come on then!' Mr Bevan ruffles Ronnie's hair. I smooth it down again. No one will pick us if he looks a proper mess. I might not want to be here, but I don't fancy us being the last ones chosen, either – the dregs in the bottom of a bottle.

We start to climb a wide track. Bushes and trees grow on either side. Ronnie asks if it's a forest. I catch Mr Bevan's eye and see his moustache twitch over his smile.

'Stop asking stupid questions,' I hiss in Ronnie's ear.

Then, up ahead, Duff's little sister drops her custard cream. She stops dead and just stays there until her face turns a greyish shade of blue. I've seen her do this lots of times before, when we've been out playing, but Mr Bevan looks horrified.

8

'What's she doing?' he asks.

'Holding her breath,' I answer. 'She can only do it for so long, then she really starts.'

'Starts what?'

'Wait for it.'

I don't know if it's got anything to do with the mountains curving all round us, but her wails are even louder here, not far off an air-raid siren. The two women rush over to her and Mrs Bevan opens her handbag. She feels around inside, pulls out a chocolate bar and snaps off a piece.

'Dairy Milk,' Ronnie groans. 'I should've dropped *my* biscuit.'

As we move off, Florence Campbell picks up the custard cream and stuffs it in her pocket. I pretend not to see. I don't think Florence can believe her luck – two biscuits in one day. I bet she's never had two biscuits in her whole life.

We keep climbing until we reach another road. We follow it round the corner until an enormous brown-brick building comes into view. It's three storeys high, bulky and strong-looking.

'I'll just catch up with Miss Goodhew and my wife at the front,' Mr Bevan says. 'You two wait by here.'

'Jimmy calls her Miss Badhew,' Ronnie says, 'because she isn't nice, so she can't be a *good* hew, can she?'

'Ronnie!' I mutter.

But Mr Bevan is laughing. 'Don't worry, Jimmy. We had nicknames for teachers when I was a boy too.'

He walks away and I can't believe I haven't been told off.

'Here we are,' he says, standing in the arched doorway. He looks really proud, like he's showing us Buckingham Palace. 'The Llanbryn Miners Institute.'

I look from Mr Bevan to the institute. They match, the way some people do with their dogs. There's something about him that says he belongs here, like he's a part of this place. But that just makes me feel even more like an outsider.

'Everyone's in the main hall. They can't wait to see you.'

The room is massive, much bigger than our school hall. It's all dark timber, polished up till it shines.

There are steps and a raised platform at the far end, a bit like a stage. The room's bursting with people all staring and muttering; surely they can't all want an evacuee? Some must be here to gawp. They sit in rows in front of the platform and, as we walk past them to the raised bit, I can feel the place swallowing us up – my little brother, all the others and me.

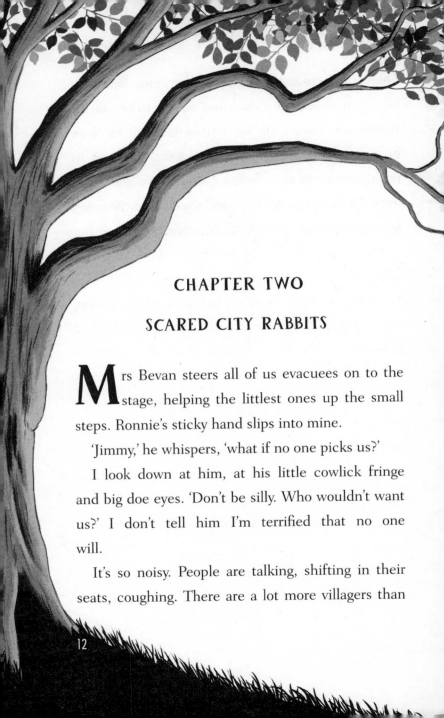

CHAPTER TWO

SCARED CITY RABBITS

Mrs Bevan steers all of us evacuees on to the stage, helping the littlest ones up the small steps. Ronnie's sticky hand slips into mine.

'Jimmy,' he whispers, 'what if no one picks us?'

I look down at him, at his little cowlick fringe and big doe eyes. 'Don't be silly. Who wouldn't want us?' I don't tell him I'm terrified that no one will.

It's so noisy. People are talking, shifting in their seats, coughing. There are a lot more villagers than evacuees. That has to be a good thing, increase our chances. If there are more of them than of us, Ronnie and me can't be left behind. Some men bring in our cases and Mrs Bevan shows where to put them on the floor in front of us. Mr Bevan steps on to the stage and the hall goes quiet. Ronnie's gripping my hand so tight it's starting to hurt but I don't care. All that matters is that someone wants us.

Mr Bevan clears his throat and says in his booming voice, 'As president of the Miners Institute and representative of the people of Llanbryn, I'd like to welcome our London visitors.'

He turns and waves an arm towards us as if we're being revealed in a magic trick. Twenty-six scared city rabbits waiting to be pulled out of a hat.

'Now, we'll do our best to get this done as quickly as possible,' Mr Bevan says, unfolding a sheet of paper. 'Miss Goodhew and the children have had a very long and tiring journey.'

I watch his eyes travel down the page. Ronnie's trembling. I drag my hand out of his and put my arm around his shoulder, pulling him close to me. He takes a big, shuddering breath and lets it out into my side. I feel the warmth of it through my jacket.

'I have the Joneses …' Mr Bevan says. Quite a few people stand up and Mr Bevan laughs but I don't get why it's funny. He carries on, 'I mean Ralph and Megan … those Joneses.'

I wonder how many Joneses are in this place. All the people, except a young-looking couple on the front row, sit down again.

'Down for one girl, I see,' Mr Bevan says.

The woman nods and points at Lillian Baker, who almost does a curtsy before moving along the stage and down the steps.

Lillian Baker first. I knew it.

Someone shuffles behind me; I look around to see Florence Campbell trying to smooth down her hair. It won't make any difference; there are so many nits it's practically moving on its own. She sees me looking and pokes out her tongue. I edge forward so no nits can jump on me. Ronnie caught them once and Nan had to rub his head with Lethane oil; he wailed for hours and coughed for weeks. No wonder the nits cleared off.

Duff and his sister go next with a woman whose nose is so far in the air I'm surprised she can see where she's going. A woman in a huge purple hat says in a loud voice that they are lucky little children. Duff glances back and gives me the thumbs up. I try to smile but it gets stuck halfway and I'm sure I must look properly daft.

Ronnie's face is still buried in my jacket. I haven't seen him like this since Mum went.

'Come on,' I whisper, 'it's like Mr Bevan said, this is an adventure, yeah?'

He sniffs and peers around the hall. Mrs Bevan smiles at him and mouths, 'Chin up.' Ronnie sticks his chin into the air and I almost laugh.

The hall's emptying quite quickly now – some evacuees go happily, some cry. A tall man with a smiley face takes the four Turners together. He and his wife hold their hands as they leave, two children each. Mr Bevan called him Dr Jenkins so I suppose he must have a big house.

About half of us have gone when a round, flushed woman wearing a flowered apron hurries in. She rolls her eyes and shakes her head like she's laughing at herself.

'Sorry, sorry!' she says, coming to the front of the hall. 'Can I go next, please, Ceri? I've had to shut the shop, see.'

My heart beats faster; she's got a shop. Even if rationing starts, I reckon an evacuee would do all right with a shopkeeper. Especially if it's a *sweet* shop.

'Come on then, Phyllis,' says Mr Bevan, checking his list. 'No preference for a boy or a girl, as long as it's just the one. Is that correct?'

Just the one. Angry tears prick at my eyes.

The woman gives us all the quick once-over and her gaze settles somewhere behind Ronnie and me.

'That girl,' she says gently.

'The one scratching her head?' Mr Bevan asks.

Florence! Florence Campbell is being picked before us! Picked before some of the other girls,

16

girls with clean faces and cardies with all the buttons on!

Florence steps off the stage. As she passes, I hear her breath quick and hard. I get a whiff of her smell; like when our old dog used to come in from the rain and dry off by the fire. The woman puts her arm around Florence. I can't believe it – no one ever touches a Campbell – you get Campbell Germs that never wash off. That's what Duff says.

Phyllis the shop woman and Florence leave the hall too.

Mr Bevan calls the next name on the list. Mrs Thomas. A fair-haired woman gets up from one of the middle rows, her eyes on Ronnie. Some people whisper and make huffing noises. Mr Bevan glares at them and she nods to him as if to say thank you, then smiles at Ronnie. He giggles.

This is it; we won't be last.

'One boy, I believe,' Mr Bevan says.

One.

I think I might really be sick, properly sick, all over my shoes sick. I just want to go home.

I'm gripping Ronnie's shoulder so tight I must be hurting him but he's just watching her. Then the woman called Mrs Thomas looks at me and I get the same smile.

'I've changed my mind, Ceri,' she says. 'We can make room for two.'

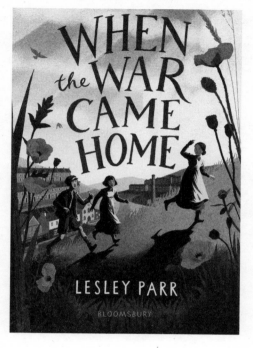

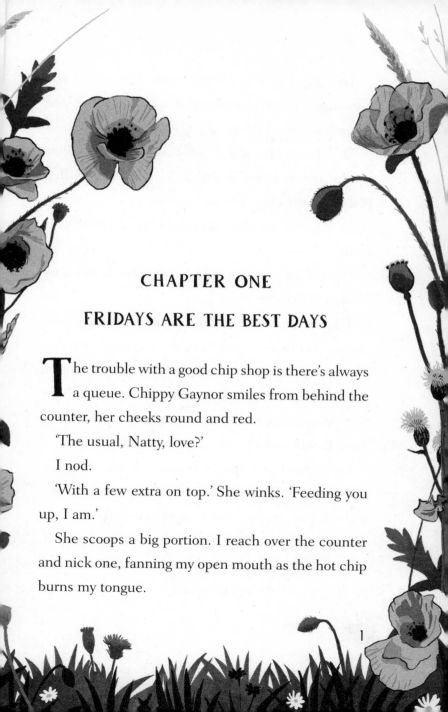

CHAPTER ONE

FRIDAYS ARE THE BEST DAYS

The trouble with a good chip shop is there's always a queue. Chippy Gaynor smiles from behind the counter, her cheeks round and red.

'The usual, Natty, love?'

I nod.

'With a few extra on top.' She winks. 'Feeding you up, I am.'

She scoops a big portion. I reach over the counter and nick one, fanning my open mouth as the hot chip burns my tongue.

'Duw, now there's a swish coat. New, is it?' she says, using tongs to pick up the cod in batter and plonk it on top of the steaming chips.

'Yes,' I say, smoothing my hand over the collar, careful not to touch it with the greasy fingers that picked up the chip. 'For my birthday.'

'Well you're a lucky dab.' She smiles. 'How's your mam?'

'Busy,' I say, thinking of all the extra hours she's worked to buy this coat.

'I know that feeling!' She grins, nodding at the queue. 'Fourpence please, love.' She holds out her plump hand. Chippy Gaynor's whole family is plump; you never go hungry if you have a chip shop. 'Your poor mam though. Gets his money's worth out of those factory girls, Litton does. Slave driver, he is.'

I pay, thank her and rush home, holding the fat, hot packet under my nose, breathing in newspaper and salt and vinegar. Fridays are the best days.

They don't have time to get cold – two doors down, above the ironmonger's and up some narrow stairs, I push open the door to our flat.

Mam's laying the table. There's three plates, one with bread and margarine on, and two glasses. Dandelion and burdock for me, stout for her. Friday night is for treats. No matter how bad things get, it's a tradition in our family. There are flowers in the bud vase in the middle of the table; they're only dog daisies picked from the lane, but they're pretty. Mam says Dad used to do it for her, but I was too small when he died to remember things like that. So now she does it for me and she always makes it nice.

'Chippy Gaynor gave us extra,' I say, kissing Mam's cheek and taking off my coat.

'Lovely.'

'I got the best bit of cod too.'

'Good girl.'

She's not looking at me, but I can see her eyes are red. She sighs as she shares out the chips. She must be tired. Like Gaynor said, Litton is a slave driver. I cut the fish not quite in half and give her the biggest end. She swaps it for the one on my plate as soon as I sit down.

'You're a growing girl. Now, tell me ... how was school?'

'Good,' I say. 'We had boiled ham with potatoes and peas.'

She smiles. 'Funny how lessons are never the first thing you tell me about.'

I shrug. 'I'm a growing girl! Arithmetic was hard, singing was easy. We had jam roly-poly for pudding. I had seconds.'

Mam laughs but it looks a bit forced. She folds a piece of bread round some chips and licks the dripping margarine off her hand. 'Natty?' I look up. 'You know how, on Monday, Lorraine Marshall had to go to the doctor?'

I nod.

'Well, as if that didn't cost her enough, Litton docked her wages for the half-hour she was gone. Half an hour! Even after I made up her quota in my dinner break.'

'You never told me that.'

She takes a big bite of her butty so she doesn't have to answer.

'Why are you telling me this now?' I ask. 'You haven't done something, have you?'

4

'Why do you think I did something?'

'Because you always do, Mam.' She'll have stuck her nose in, gone on about workers' rights and fairness and, if she can manage to fit it in, votes for women too. Champion of the underdog, that's my mother.

'Well, Natty, people need to see a doctor if they're ill without the fear of losing money.' She looks at her plate. 'So I called a meeting today, to see what can be done about Litton ... and ... he sacked me.'

'He *what*?'

She puts down her knife and fork, and rubs her forehead. 'It's just not right how he treats people. He needs to understand how it is for us. For the workers.'

'But you always say he's never had to struggle for anything in his life! He inherited that factory, so why would he listen now? It's pointless.'

'Standing up for what you believe in is never pointless. Especially now. The war is over. It's the twenties, things are changing.'

'But the only thing that changed was you getting the sack.'

'Eat your tea before it gets cold.'

I slowly peel the batter off my fish, not looking at her.

'There's something else,' Mam says. 'But it's going to be all right because I have a plan.' She takes a big breath. 'If we can't find the rent this week, Mr Tipton will throw us out ... I ... I got a bit behind, see.'

Oh no, not again. I don't want to move *again*.

'How? How can you get behind? You always say a roof over our heads is more important than anything!' I point to the fish and chips. 'Why would you give me money for this if we didn't have the rent?'

Mam's quiet. She's looking at her and Dad's wedding photograph on the cabinet. Friday night supper was something else Dad used to do. That's why. But things have been tight before – why is it so bad this time? Her eyes move to my coat hanging on the hook by the door.

And suddenly I'm furious. But not with her, with myself. If I hadn't stopped outside Nicholls every time we passed, looking up at that coat in the window, if I hadn't grown so fast and always had extra helpings of school dinners, I'd still be in my old coat. It would have patched. We could have let the seams out again.

'We can take it back,' I whisper, the words scratching over the lump in my throat. 'My coat, we can take it back.'

'It won't be enough, sweetheart.'

'So you picked a fight with Litton, when it wasn't even your fight to have, when you knew we were behind on the rent?'

'Lorraine Marshall's got her girl home with the babies, her being a war widow. But, Natty –' she leans across the table – 'Like I said, I have a plan. We won't be out on the street. I wrote to your Aunty Mary and Uncle Dewi last week.'

'Why?'

'When your dad died, they were good to us. They've always said if we need anything, I only have to ask.'

'Ask for what? Not money! Mam, that's shaming!'

'No, no. Not money. Just a place to stay until I can find a new job—'

'But don't they live in Ynysfach?' I drop my fork and it clatters on the plate. Mam winces.

'Yes, love, that's where we're going. I got a letter back this morning.'

I frown. 'And you wrote to them *last week*? But you lost your job today?'

Mam shuffles in her seat. 'I knew it was coming. Litton was just looking for a way to get rid of me.'

'And you gave him one. You knew we were behind on the rent and you still had to make trouble!'

Mam looks at her plate for a few seconds, then pushes her chair back. 'I'm going for a walk.'

'But your food!'

'I'll have it after.'

'Cold?' I say. 'Because there's not enough coal to heat the oven. Lorraine Marshall can look after herself, Mam. What about us?'

She doesn't look at me, just leaves me at the table.

'What about *us*?' I shout after her, but she's gone.

So much for Fridays being the best days.

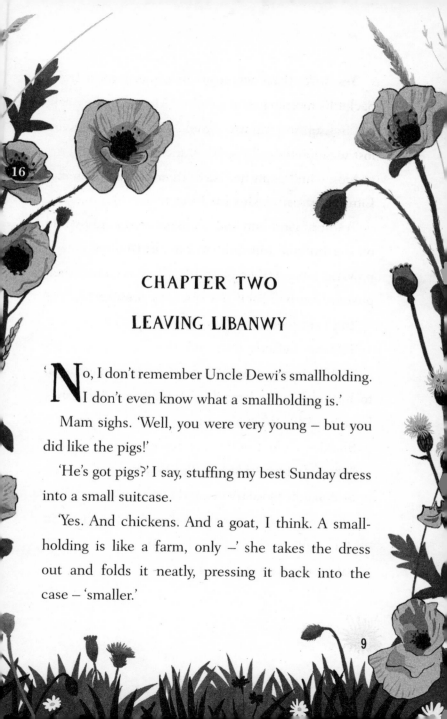

CHAPTER TWO

LEAVING LIBANWY

'No, I don't remember Uncle Dewi's smallholding. I don't even know what a smallholding is.'

Mam sighs. 'Well, you were very young – but you did like the pigs!'

'He's got pigs?' I say, stuffing my best Sunday dress into a small suitcase.

'Yes. And chickens. And a goat, I think. A smallholding is like a farm, only –' she takes the dress out and folds it neatly, pressing it back into the case – 'smaller.'

Aunty Mary said we must come as soon as possible. So here we are, four days after Mam got the sack, packing up our things. Again. But this time we're moving away from Libanwy – and my school and my friends – and going to live with smelly animals and some relatives I don't even know.

'It's very kind of them to allow us to stay while we get back on our feet, and it won't be for long. I promise.'

'Like you promised not to cause problems at the factory?'

She goes stiff for a second, then carries on in an even jollier voice. 'You won't get to see your cousin Sara though, she's a maid in Cardiff now, but Huw's at home still, and Nerys is your age – that'll be nice, won't it?'

Why do grown-ups always think you'll get on with people just because they're the same age as you?

Mam sighs again and closes the lid of the case. 'Sit on this, will you? It'll never close otherwise.'

I thud down on it, extra hard.

*

I wish we didn't have to walk past the factory to get to the bus stop. And that the bus wasn't going at the end of the factory dinner break, because there are all Mam's old workmates, standing on the steps waiting to go back in.

We try to hurry past but it's no use. A woman in a blue headscarf steps out of the little crowd, pointing at our suitcases. It's Lorraine Marshall.

'Ffion, is this because of me?' she asks.

Mam slows but keeps walking.

'No, Lorraine. It was a long time coming.'

The factory doors open and there's Dennis Litton, looking like a smug cockerel. He scans the crowd until his eyes rest on Mam. 'You no longer work here, Mrs Lydiate. You need to remove yourself from my premises.'

'I'm not on your premises,' Mam says, stepping forward so her toe is right on the edge of where the steps start.

Oh Mam, what are you doing?

'If *this lot* want to put up with your tyranny –' she nods towards the factory girls but keeps her eyes on him – 'more fool them. Me? I'm glad to see the back of you.'

The bus is pulling up, so I run and get the driver to wait. Mam strolls across the road, her head held high.

'She won't be a minute now,' I say.

The driver turns around in his seat. 'What's going on there then?'

'Nothing.'

I climb the steps, annoyed with myself for feeling a little bit proud of her when I'm supposed to be cross.

I stare out of the window as we bounce along the long road to Ynysfach. The tree-covered drop into the valley is so deep I can't see the river at the bottom. And then we're climbing even higher, the driver forcing his bus up and up over the mountain. Up and down, up and down, all the way to Uncle Dewi's.

Mam offers me a crumpled paper bag. 'Mint humbug?'

I take one. 'Thanks.'

'Oh, you're speaking to me then?'

I look away and roll my eyes. She keeps on. 'It's a nice afternoon for a bus ride.'

She's trying to make the best of it, but I'm not going to join in and treat this like some sort of jaunt. We've just left the nicest flat we've ever lived in and the only village I know. And it's all her fault.

'I remember Nerys now,' I say, glancing at her. Before she can answer I add, 'She was annoying.'

I pop the humbug in my mouth, fold my arms and look out of the window again.

Two more humbugs later, the bus pulls up opposite some bushes and flowerbeds set behind railings. There's a sign saying *Ynysfach Park*.

'Must be our stop,' Mam says. We shuffle along the aisle with our cases and step down on to the pavement, just as a nurse and two soldiers in Hospital Blues and khaki caps come towards us. The nurse is pushing one in a wheelchair; the other is really young, not much older than me. Almost too young to have fought in the war. And too young to look so sad. He's very fair, in a gingery-blond sort of way, even his eyelashes are pale. I realise my suitcase is in the way

13

of the wheelchair so I go to move it just as the younger soldier reaches out as if to help. But his hand shakes and shakes, so he pulls it back. We lock eyes for a second that feels like forever; like we're both unsure what to do next. There's something about the way he is. It's like how I feel.

Lost.

'It's all right, I've got it,' I say as the others and Mam say hello, then the soldiers and nurse cross the road over to the park.

A passenger calls out for the bus to get a move on, and the driver leans out of his seat and glowers up the aisle. 'Have some respect, mun!' Then he faces the road again and makes a salute before pulling off.

Mam looks around. 'I don't think this is right, there are meant to be shops. We must have got off too early.'

I huff, but say nothing, just pick up my suitcase and trudge down the hill.

ABOUT THE AUTHOR

Lesley Parr is the author of three novels for children. Her debut, *The Valley of Lost Secrets*, was published in 2021 and was both a Waterstones Book of the Month and longlisted for the CILIP Carnegie Medal. It won the Tir na n-Og Award, the King's School Chester Book Award and the North Somerset Teachers' Book Award, as well as being shortlisted for many others. Lesley grew up in South Wales and now lives in England with her husband. She shares her time between writing stories, teaching at a primary school and tutoring adults. Apart from books, rugby union is her favourite thing in the world, especially if Wales is winning.

@WelshDragonParr

lesleyparr.com